SPIRIT WOLF

BY

MARK W. HOLDREN

ISBN: 0-9760648-0-4

Library of Congress Control Number: 2003097971

Cover design by Richard C. Burandt and M & P Design Group.

Illustrations by Richard C. Burandt

Powell Hill Press
6470 Powell Hill Road
Naples, NY 14512
www. Spiritwolf.info

Printed in the United States of America

Dedication

TO GARY MICHAEL HOLDREN

Acknowledgements

No book is written alone. The author expresses his heartfelt thanks and appreciation to Rene Latorre and the Rochester Association for the Blind and Visually Impaired. Rene's guidance, patience, and understanding lit the way. Hugh Crossin's wise eye, Todd Brady's keen ear, and Dick Burandt's talented hand helped bring **Spirit Wolf** to life.

Prologue

You have one new message.

"Hello, Jason. It's Noah Boone. I've got bad news. Charlie Two Shirts is dead. He told me a week ago he was near the end of his last carry, what he called his path to the Great Long House. Bushy and I found him this morning on Loon Island. He was sitting under that twisted cedar on the point, frozen clear through to the bone. Looks like he walked out there a couple nights ago, pulled that old muskrat cap over his eyes, and let the cold gnaw at him and his cancer until they both were dead.

"What happened here at Wolf River Lodge that Christmas in 1987 is still a matter of spirited debate. Most swear it was all just a coincidence. Others, well, they're not so sure. But you know the magic that can flow from these mountains, thanks to Charlie—and Lucas of course. Give us a call when you get this message."

Chapter One

"...if we hope for what we do not see, we wait for it with patience.

Book of Romans

"Dad, is it snowing?" Jason Quinn cried out. "I can feel wet stuff on my nose."

Todd Quinn looked over his shoulder. His nine-year-old son was about twenty feet behind him, shuffling across the snow-swept parking lot.

"It sure is," he replied.

Jason smiled, but his elf-like brown eyes looked empty and cold.

"It'll be a white Christmas in Wolf River for sure," his mother said.

Jason heard her slam the car trunk.

"Abbie, make sure the car's locked," his father shouted back, "and turn on the anti-theft alarm."

"Who'll hear it?" she asked. "We passed the last signs of civilization three miles back."

Jason wiped his nose with the back of his glove, then pulled his stocking cap down over his ears, covering the five- inch crimson scar still etched across the back of his head.

He guessed from the echo of their voices that he was halfway between the car and the old railroad depot. His father was headed to the depot with their duffel bags, his footsteps puncturing the frozen snow like plate glass.

"Hey, Dad," he shouted, "are there any trains?"

His father kicked the snow from the depot's steps with his boot and tossed the bags down in a heap.

"There's an old caboose, a couple of beat-up passenger cars— that's about it."

Jason listened while his father counted the pickup trucks, vans, and SUV's—maybe a dozen—scattered around the depot's parking lot. Most were hitched to empty flatbed trailers.

"There isn't much left of Wolf River Station, Jason. Just the depot and five ramshackle wood-frame buildings."

His father described the Lost Moose Bed & Breakfast, right across the street, which was for sale. Its windows were boarded shut,

2

its porch roof caved in from neglect and several feet of snow. There were long icicles hanging from the depot's dry-rotted eaves.

"They look like frozen tears," his father mused.

There was a weather-beaten metal sign that read **Whistle Stop Cafe**; Jason could hear it groan from its rusted chains like a condemned man swinging in the wind. And there was a hand-lettered cardboard sign duct-taped to the front window:

See you Memorial Day Weekend!

Molly & Lefty

"What's inside?" Jason asked.

His father looked through a window and described the interior. There was a small dining room. The walls were decorated with signal switches, old railroad posters, and faded photographs. He could see a bar at the far end of the room. There was a **GENNY ON TAP** sign hanging over the cash register.

"Boy, could I go for a Genny now," his father said, laughing.

Jason had found his way to the depot steps.

"What's so funny, Dad?"

"Nothing, Jason," his father replied, "just thinking of an old TV commercial." He stepped off the porch. "Looks like this is where those snowmobiles were headed."

"What do you mean?" Jason asked.

"There's a large, official-looking sign in front of the station," his father explained. "And there's a color-keyed map. I'm guessing the old rail bed is the main snowmobile trail. It's marked in yellow. There are connecting green and red trails that twist around what appears to be three lakes and several smaller ponds."

Some parts of the map were marked **Wild Forest**, others as **Wilderness** and **Primitive** areas. The latter was clearly restricted: **MOTOR VEHICLES PROHIBITTED.**

Jason was already shivering. He couldn't remember ever being so cold. But he was glad to be out of the car.

The three-hour ride from Rochester to Old Forge, where they'd stopped for lunch, hadn't been bad. Even the Wolf River Station Road had been kind of fun; sitting in the backseat had been like riding a roller coaster.

But with his mother constantly shouting, "Slow down!" the whole way there and his father swearing at the snowmobiles that roared past them on both sides of the road, he wondered if either one of them had really wanted to come.

It was his mother's idea.

"Discover the magic of an old-fashioned Christmas at Wolf River Lodge," she read aloud from the Sunday newspaper one morning. "Explore our wilderness sanctuary—ten miles from the nearest road."

"If there's no road," his father asked, "how in hell are we supposed to get there—by dogsled?"

"Well, sort of," his mother replied. "They pick you up at an old railroad station and take you to the lodge in a horse-driven sleigh."

Jason knew the trip wouldn't be easy for him. He was just learning to get around on his own, and that was at home. At the lodge, everything would be new. But he was looking forward to the adventure.

His mother thought it would be good for them all to get away, to try and put the last six months behind them somehow.

But even he knew that was impossible. Everything had changed for him. For all of them. His mother cried a lot. Oh, she tried to hide it, but he could hear her. And he could sense his father blamed himself for the accident; if he'd been there, it wouldn't have happened.

No one was to blame, but Jason was beginning to feel like he was a burden his parents couldn't handle.

Todd Quinn watched his wife carry their last bags from the car. Her thick wool slacks and long black leather coat disguised her finch-like frame.

Thank God for Abbie, he thought. *She's handling it better than I ever will. Sure she's overly protective, hovering over him all the time. But, hey, she's his mother.*

He tried to smile, but all he could do was bite his lip.

Better give her a hand, he thought.

He drew the collar of his coat around his bulldog neck and spun into the snow that swirled in a ghost-like tango across the deserted parking lot.

"Jeez, it's cold," he muttered.

He recalled how warm it had been the second Saturday in April. How could he ever forget?

He was in the garage that morning, trying to start the damn lawn mower. He'd never had to cut the grass so early in the spring.

Maybe there is something to this global warming nonsense after all, he thought.

He was about to head for Home Depot in search of a new spark plug when the phone rang. It was a Monroe County Sheriff's Deputy. "Your son's been hurt," Sgt. Glenn Michaels said matter-of-factly. "Jason's in an ambulance. You should get to Rochester General."

"That damn skateboard." Todd had muttered as he hung up. He'd seen Jason heading down the street with the rainbow-colored board over his shoulder earlier that morning. He didn't have his helmet.

Kick flipping his board in the high school parking lot, Jason had simply lost it. The back of his head struck the edge of the concrete curb first. A friend said it sounded like a rifle shot.

When Todd and Abbie arrived at the hospital, doctors had already begun to put Jason into what they called an induced coma, to rest the brain, they said. A day later they removed a portion of Jason's skull to reduce the brain's swelling. It would be three

6

traumatic weeks before he regained consciousness. Doctors would later replace his skull section. It would heal completely. Jason's brain was another matter. The neurologist called it a cortical condition. He said the occipital lobes of Jason's brain were severely damaged. Surgery was not an option.

"Jason's eyes are fine," Dr. Robert Kerr explained, "but the sight center of his brain no longer functions."

"What are you trying to tell us, doctor?" Todd asked, with Abbie crying at his side.

"I'm sorry. Jason is blind."

"My God, he's only nine," Abbie screamed.

"Over time, some healing may occur," Dr. Kerr said, trying to calm her. "But I can't make any promises. Injuries like this have a mind of their own."

Todd hadn't noticed that Abbie was beginning to share his doubts about the trip. She met him in the middle of the parking lot, where she dropped the duffel bags at his feet.

"I hope this is the right place," she muttered, rolling her saucer-like brown eyes and laughing.

The cold was clawing hard on her husband's blade-like nose. It was wet and pink, like a slab of salmon hanging between his icy blue eyes. He was wearing a thick green wool cap tied beneath his chin. She thought he looked like the world's tallest gnome. She watched him trudge back toward the station.

Maybe this trip will be too much for all of us, she worried. *It's been just seven months since Jason's accident. He's made extraordinary progress, thanks to his therapist, Bill Robinson. There are bound to be problems, what with the new surroundings, strangers.*

She hoped Todd's office would leave him alone. This was supposed to be their Christmas vacation. But there was no place to hide with a cell phone and pager clipped to his belt.

Todd R. Quinn, eastern regional sales manager for the country's largest medical equipment marketer, was always on call. The Cleveland Clinic, one of his largest accounts, had already tracked him down this morning via the car phone. One of their cardiac surgeons needed two of Todd's new mechanical heart valves—in six hours. Todd had worked the phone as they drove east from Rochester on the New York State Thruway. He solved the crisis somewhere between Geneva and Weedsport.

His job had always involved travel, but since Jason's accident he'd been staying out longer, attending more so—called symposiums—a euphemism adopted by the medical supply industry for sophisticated sales pitches to doctors and hospital purchasing agents. He said weekend travel came with the territory, but his wife suspected he was beginning to run from the cruel hand they'd been dealt. He was drinking more. It wasn't a problem, yet. But he was kicking off the cocktail hour at five instead of six. And that was when he was home.

She reached the depot steps and took her husband's hand. "I know this was my idea," she whispered, "but I hope this isn't too much for Jason, for all of us."

"I can hear you, Mom," Jason shouted. He was sitting on a snow bank at the edge of the trail. "Don't worry about me. I'll be fine. You'll see."

He reached for one of the Snickers bars he'd squirreled away in his coat pocket. He wondered what advice Bill might have for him now.

"Listen to your heart," he would probably say. "It will always show you the way."

Jason remembered how angry he'd been when he came home from the hospital. A woman from the Association for the Blind and Visually Impaired was waiting for him. She wanted to make sure he had everything he needed. A rehabilitation specialist was next. She began to teach him how to manage for himself. Bill Robinson came the third week. He was an orientation and mobility instructor. The OMI, his father called him.

"You might find this hard to believe," Bill began, "but your anger will help you learn faster."

Jason didn't like Bill at first. He was too demanding.

What did he know about being blind?

They weren't making much progress. Then Bill began taking him on short walks: first just around the neighborhood, then to Mendon Ponds Park, a nearby nature sanctuary. Jason found his way along the trails by holding onto Bill's elbow.

9

"What do you hear?" Bill would ask. "Where is the sound coming from? What do you smell? What do you think it means?"

Gradually, Jason began to see in a new way. Bill started walking behind him, encouraging him to find his own way.

"Life is going to be more physically demanding," he would say. "There will be times when you feel hopelessly lost. You'll fall over something. You'll trip. Don't panic. Get up. Think your way through the problem. Learn to trust the sounds, the smells, and the feel of things to tell you where you are."

Then Bill surprised him with a gift: a CD collection called **Wilderness Voices.** There were croaks and screeches, hoots and cries of more than sixty birds and animals. It wasn't long before Jason was singing himself, intoning the **dee-dee-dee** of the chickadee, or the **pip-pip-pip** of the wood thrush.

Their adventures lengthened to afternoon-long affairs. Jason's favorite trail in the park circled Deep Pond. His keen ear quickly caught the **cluck-cluck** of the northern leopard frog; the banjo-like call of the green frog; and the **jug-o-rum, jug-o-rum** of the bullfrogs that lived in the pond's shallows.

His confidence grew, especially when he was outdoors. Somehow he felt comforted by the natural sounds around him. He began to attack his lessons with a fierce sense of determination. He learned to walk with a cane. Bill showed him how to sweep the three-foot long rod in front of him in one direction while stepping forward on the opposite foot.

Jason's parents were learning their lessons as well.

10

"Never walk away from Jason without telling him," Bill told them. "And don't ever shout at him; Jason isn't deaf, you know. Don't push him or shove him. Let him take your elbow and walk just a step behind you."

Bill taught him to walk from room to room by listening to the sound of the walls. He called it "echolocation."

"You will learn to walk down the street by listening to the sound of buildings," he said. "It's like listening to air. Sound is all around us. When it changes, that means there is something between you and the sound."

Bill circled him, clapping in different locations, challenging him to point in the direction of the sound. He learned to listen for people walking, doors opening—little sounds he'd never paid attention to before. He remembered which rooms were noisy, like the kitchen and dining room, and which rooms were quieter, like the living room and den. He was learning to see the world through his ears instead of his eyes.

But now, sitting on the snow bank, he was blinded by the silence. He took another bite of his Snickers bar. The wind was spooking him. For all he knew, there was nothing out there but snow. The darkness made him feel the coldness even more. He finished off the candy bar. He wondered what it would be like to open Christmas presents he couldn't see.

"When's the sleigh coming, Mom?"

"It's almost three o'clock. If it's on time, it should be here any minute."

Jason couldn't see the plum-colored clouds that were rolling in horizontal sheets across the cold, gray December sky. He couldn't read the uneasiness in his mother's eyes as she stared up the trail. He couldn't feel his father's impatience as he paced the loading platform. He couldn't possibly know what was waiting for him, hidden for now by his blindness and by the blowing snow.

Chapter Two

Jason heard it first. He slid down the snow bank and stood in the middle of the trail.

"It's coming," he shouted, pointing up the trail. "I hear bells ringing."

His mother squinted into the snow. There was a splash of color against an otherwise bone-white canvas. She jumped off the platform and ran to Jason's side.

"I can see two horses' heads," she told him.

There was steam pouring from their nostrils, like smoke from the coal-fired locomotives that once rumbled up and down the now-abandoned tracks.

"There it is!" she shouted. "Oh, get the camera, Todd. What a Christmas card this will make."

She could see the driver clearly now. He was an immense man, who appeared to float between the horses' gigantic heads.

"Jason, the man driving the sleigh looks like Santa himself. He's wearing a red-and-black-checkered wool jacket. He has a thick fur cap pulled down over his ears. His beard is yellowish white, like a great polar bear."

Todd found his camera and squeezed off a few shots.

"Hand me the camera, Todd," she said. I'll get a picture of you and Jason. Wave at the driver."

Jason could feel the horses' hoof beats through the soles of his boots.

They must be huge, he thought.

His father told him they were a matched pair, butterscotch in color. Their manes were misty gray.

"Jason, I'll bet they weigh over a thousand pounds," he said.

"Dad, what's the sleigh look like?"

"It's green with gold trim, maybe twelve feet long, Jason. It's decorated with bright silver bells. There are two runners on either side, and it has two high-backed seats."

Now Jason had a good picture of the sleigh. And if the driver looked like Santa, well, Santa he would be. He tried to put faces on people, guessing what they looked like from their voices, their touch, the words they used.

14

He felt his mother easing him off to the side. He could smell the horses now. They must be close.

"Whoa there, Jeb. Whoa, Joe," he heard the driver bellow.

The horses took two more steps, snorted loudly, and stopped. Jason had already forgotten how cold he was.

"Now I bet you're the Quinn family," the driver called out.

He jumped down from the driver's seat onto the platform, his quickness belying his three-hundred-pound frame. He gave each horse a scratch behind the ear and then tied them off to a corner post.

"The name's Barnes—Wilfred Sullivan Barnes. Most folks just call me Bushy."

He looked to be in his mid-forties. He was moon-faced, his cheeks wind-burnt and raw. His emerald eyes appeared to sparkle through the snow. He peeled off his right glove and squeezed Todd's hand.

"Pardon the iron grip," he quipped.

Todd winced. He managed a weak smile when Bushy let go.

"Mrs. Quinn," Bushy continued, removing his cap.

Abbie spotted the earring immediately. It was gold and shaped like a fishhook.

Bushy dropped to a knee and wrapped his gloved hands around her son's shoulders. "And you must be Jason," he said.

When Abby had called the lodge to make their reservation, she'd asked if bringing their blind son would be a problem. The answer was "definitely not." Bushy's friendly behavior hammered the point home.

"How are you doing, young man?" Bushy asked.

"Fine," Jason replied. He couldn't see him, but he felt very small, being squeezed, albeit gently, between what felt like enormous hands. "Mom says you look like Santa Claus."

"Well, I suppose if old Jeb and Joe could fly, we could give Santa a hand on Christmas Eve," Bushy laughed.

Jason had never heard such a laugh. It was thick and sweet, like maple syrup. Jason felt Bushy pat him on the head, then heard the man's knees crack. Jason guessed he was standing up.

"You know what Vince Lombardi said, eh, Mr. Quinn?

Jason's father rose to the bait.

"No, what did he say?"

"The knee, always the knee."

Jason didn't get it, but his father laughed, so he guessed it was a joke.

"Mr. Quinn, let's get your luggage on board and get started."

"Bushy, be careful with that one!" Jason heard his mother shout. "It's full of Christmas presents."

"From the heft of it, Mrs. Quinn, I'd say we're doing Santa a favor."

Jason felt Bushy take his hand.

"Say hello to Jeb and Joe. They won't bite."

Jason reached out and touched what he guessed was a big nose.

Jeb let loose with a loud snort.

Startled, Jason jumped back, but he was laughing.

"Well, I guess that means we're ready to go," Bushy announced. "Jason, you can ride up front with me."

His parents climbed into the back.

"There's extra blankets under the front seat if you need 'em," Bushy added.

He untied the horses, gave each a pat on the snout, then climbed into the sleigh.

"Ready, Jason?" he asked.

"Yes, sir, Mr. Barnes."

"Now don't you be giving me that Mr. Barnes business. Just call me Bushy, okay, partner?"

"Okay, Bushy," Jason nodded and smiled.

He pulled his blanket up around his shoulders. He already liked this loud, funny man, although he wasn't sure why.

Bushy kind of reminds me of Bill, he thought. *Bill's the only real friend I've had since the accident. The guys at school, they came around for a while, but there just isn't much to talk about anymore.*

Abbie took her husband's hand. "I think Jason's found a new friend," she whispered.

"He's a character, that's for sure," Todd replied. "He's probably not the last one we'll meet on this trip of yours."

Bushy settled into his seat and snapped the reins. "Giddap, Jeb. Giddap, Joe."

The sleigh lurched ahead as the horses stepped away from the platform. They turned in a wide circle, then headed north up the trail. Abbie took one last look at their car. The sun was sliding behind a bank of menacingly dark clouds. She pulled her blanket up around her.

"Bushy, tell us something about this sleigh," Todd said. "It looks like a real antique."

"Well, it's not a sleigh, actually," he began, talking over his right shoulder. "It's a bobsled. The front runners are called the lead bob. Them in the back, that's the tail bob. When you put a deck on 'em, you got a bobsled. They call this a family bob 'cause of the sideboards."

Todd wrapped his arm around Abbie's shoulder. "This guy is right out of central casting," he whispered.

Abbie nodded. "Say, uh, Bushy. I couldn't help but notice that earring. It's a fishhook, isn't it?"

"That's right, Mrs. Quinn. You gotta be a promoter, know what I mean?"

Abbie gave her husband a quizzical look.

"I do some guiding," Bushy continued. "We've still got some good trout water up here, despite the acid-rain problem. A good guide's got to be an entertainer. The earring is all part of my act, so to speak," he added with a laugh.

"What's the acid-rain problem?" Todd asked.

"Dirty, coal-fired power plants in the Midwest have turned some of our lakes into vinegar," Bushy barked back. "Believe it or not, the junk in their smokestacks drifts back here. Noah Boone—he and his wife, Kate, own the lodge—has been fighting it for years. I don't want to get political, but with the way things are in Washington now, you can bet things will just get worse."

Abbie peeked from beneath the blanket she now had wrapped almost over her head. "Mr. Barnes—I mean, Bushy—how long will it take us to get to the lodge?" She stamped her feet to warm them up as she looked worriedly at Jason, who was bearing the brunt of the wind.

"Oh, about an hour and change should do it."

She dug beneath the seat for another blanket. "Jason, how are you doing up there? Are you warm enough?"

Jason wasn't thinking about the cold. He was listening to the sled's runners slice through the snow. He welcomed the wind against his face. It was like riding his bike. He missed flying down Parson's Hill on his way to school.

We must be riding through a pine woods, he thought. *It smells like Christmas trees.*

"Jason, why don't you drive for a while," Bushy said matter-of-factly.

"Who, me?" Jason replied.

"Sure, nothing to it. You hold the reins like this."

Bushy folded Jason's fingers around the thick leather straps.

"Keep your palms up and thumbs pointing out toward Jeb and Joe. This way you got a good grip."

"But I can't...I can't see where we're going," Jason pleaded.

"You keep a firm grip," Bushy replied, "and I'll keep a clear eye."

Jason cautiously took the reins. There was a gentle pull to the right, then the left. His heart was pounding. He remembered those runaway stagecoaches he used to see on TV.

"Hey, you guys!" he shouted to his parents. "How do I look?

"Terrific," his father replied. "Turn around so I can get a picture."

He snapped the shot and then groused under his breath, "Pictures? I'm taking pictures Jason will never see. Pictures that will do nothing but remind us of what we've lost."

He looked around. They were passing through a thick stand of white pines, which gradually gave way to a mix of maple and yellow birch. The sun continued to slip in and out of the darkening clouds. Abbie had pulled the blankets nearly over her head. Black, bony-fingered shadows were stretching out from the trees and across the trail.

He blew on his hands and grimaced.

"Now that I've got a free hand," Bushy called back, "who'd like some hot cider? I've got a thermos full under the seat here somewhere."

"Sounds great," Abbie replied from beneath her blankets.

"You wouldn't have something a little stronger under that seat, would you, good buddy?" Todd asked.

"Sorry, Mr. Quinn, you'll have to wait till we get to the lodge."

"I wasn't a Boy Scout for nothing," Todd said, turning to Abbie. "Always be prepared."

He began digging through a duffel bag for his quart of Canadian Club.

Bushy filled two steaming stoneware mugs with cider. Todd's was soon sufficiently spiked.

"I've never had hot cider before," Jason said.

"Ah, you'll love it. Really hits the spot on a cold winter's day," Bushy replied. "Here, let me take the reins for a minute."

He placed a half-filled mug in Jason's hands. "Just give her a sip."

Jason tentatively lifted the mug to his lips. "Hey, that's good."

"Cinnamon's the secret, my lad," Bushy said. "Just a touch."

Jason felt a hot rush as the warm liquid settled into his stomach. He was beginning to like Bushy a lot.

He doesn't talk to me the way my parents' friends do, he thought. *They just feel sorry for me. It's in their voices.* Jason hoped he'd see Bushy a lot while they were at the lodge. Then he laughed a dark laugh, all to himself. *See him? I can't see him. I wonder why I keep thinking that word?*

"Say, Bushy, are you a native?" his father asked. "Did you grow up around here?"

"You bet," Bushy replied.

Jason waited for more, but apparently that was all Bushy was going to say.

"I assume the trail we're on is the old railroad line," his father said.

21

"That's right," Bushy began. "William Seward Webb built it in the 1890's. It was called the Mohawk and Malone then. Webb was a doctor. Made a fortune on Wall Street. Married Lila Vanderbilt. Her father was William Vanderbilt, the railroad tycoon. Webb bought nearly 200,000 acres around Smith Lake, which he renamed Lake Lila. Built a big lodge there. Called the whole place Nehasane Park. That's an Indian word meaning beaver crossing a river on a log, or something close to that."

"Is the lodge still there?" Jason's mother asked.

"Nope," Bushy continued. "The state bought most of Webb's property a few years back. They classified Lake Lila a Primitive Area. That means no buildings. So the DEC boys—that's the Department of Environmental Conservation—they burned the lodge to the ground. Part of Nehasane Station is still standing. It's about twenty miles up the line from here. Back in Webb's day, the railroad wouldn't sell anyone a ticket to Nehasane Station unless they were a guest of the Webb's and could prove it.

Todd took another sip from his cider. The Canadian Club was beginning to do its job.

"Pass that thermos back, would you, Bushy?" he asked.

He topped off his mug and added another shot.

"This should get me to the lodge," he muttered, settling back into his blankets. "Maybe this won't be so bad after all."

"So how long has the railroad been shut down?" he asked.

"The New York Central ran through here until 1965," Bushy replied. "They got it running again for the Lake Placid Olympics in 1980 but couldn't make a go of it after the games."

"We saw some old train cars in Thendara this morning," Abbie said.

"That's the Adirondack Scenic Railroad," Bushy replied. "They've restored a few miles of track out of Old Forge. Same thing up in Saranac Lake. There's talk of opening the whole line again. That could be a whole bunch of trouble for us."

"What do you mean?" Todd asked.

"We use the tracks. That's how we get most of our supplies to the lodge. We've got a couple of pickup trucks with train wheels. Run 'em right on the tracks."

Abbie poked her head out from beneath a mountain of blankets. "You've got to be kidding."

"We ride down to Wolf River Station. Keep a van there to drive to Old Forge, or wherever. We also get supplies by boat from Lou's Landing at the west end of the lake. Come winter, Jeb and Joe haul most everything in. The small stuff we can bring by snowmobile."

Abbie shook her head in disbelief. "I can't imagine how anyone could live so isolated from the rest of the world. There can't be a mall within a hundred miles of here."

"Well, Mrs. Quinn," Bushy said, looking back over his shoulder, "let me put it this way: when a crow flies over these parts, it better carry its own lunch bucket." He winked and laughed.

"Speaking of these parts," Todd began, "I saw a sign before we got to Old Forge: **Welcome to the Adirondack Park**. But there are cottages and cabins, small businesses all along Route 28. Old Forge is almost a booming metropolis. Where is the park, anyway?"

"When you passed that sign, south of White Lake, you crossed the Blue Line. That's the way the park's boundaries are drawn on most maps. The Adirondack Park encompasses six million acres. That's larger than Yellowstone, Yosemite, and Grand Canyon National Parks combined, or about the size of New Hampshire."

Todd threw back the rest of his cider and wondered about asking for more. He didn't have to.

"The park was created by the state in 1892 to protect the Adirondacks from clear-cut loggers," Bushy continued.

"They have spotted owls up here, too?" Todd asked with a sly laugh.

"No spotted owls, Mr. Quinn. They were clear-cutting here in the 1850's for lumber, charcoal, and the tanning industry. It was a real mess."

"The tanning industry?" Abbie asked.

"There were tanneries all over the Adirondacks in those days," he continued. "They cut down the hemlock trees, stripped off the bark for its tannin, then left the trees to rot on the ground. Sort of like how the buffalo were slaughtered out West. Hunters stripped their hides, then left the carcasses behind."

"How awful," Abbie remarked.

"There's plenty up here worth protecting: more than 3,000 lakes and ponds, some 15,000 miles of rivers and streams," Bushy said.

"How many people live up here?" Todd asked. "I mean, year-round."

"Oh, around 130,000," Bushy continued. "Half the land in the park is public land, protected forever as wild by the state constitution. Development of the rest—the private land—is regulated by the Adirondack Park Agency. Rules are pretty strict, most of the time. Things get a little dicey, though, when some of the natives think the state is pushing them too hard."

Jason was still thinking about dead trees and buffalo lying all over the ground when he heard something rumbling.

"What's that noise?" he asked.

"You got a good ear, partner," Bushy replied. "We'll be crossing the Wolf River just up ahead. What you're hearing is Cascade Falls. Drops a good seventy-five feet. There's a deep hole at the bottom. Full of brownies."

"Brownies?" Jason asked.

"Trout, my boy. Brown trout. Charlie Two Shirts and I got a couple of seven pounders out of that hole last summer. I call 'em football browns, being so fat and all."

"Charlie...Two Shirts?" his father asked.

"Charlie being an Indian and all—"

Jason nearly dropped his cider. "A real Indian?"

"Full-blooded Mohawk," Bushy replied. "Like I was saying, being an Indian and living in a caboose—"

Jason's mother sprung from beneath her blankets again. "An Indian named Charlie Two Shirts...who lives in caboose?"

"She was tore up pretty good, the caboose I mean, in a derailment back in the fifties," Bushy continued. "Charlie picked up the pieces and hauled them up to Chapel Pond. Put it all back together. Got a fine little house."

Jason had forgotten about the waterfall. "Where did he get a name like Charlie Two Shirts?" he asked.

"Well, I'm getting to that," Bushy continued. "Being the only Indian around, and livin' like he does, people are naturally curious, always stoppin' by his place, specially in the summer. Now Charlie's a right personal fella, most of the time. That's when he hangs an old green shirt off the lantern on the back of the caboose. That means it's okay to come on in. When Charlie wants to be alone, he hangs out a red shirt."

"Is Charlie Two Shirts some kind of hermit?" Jason's mother asked.

"Oh, no. Charlie helps out around the lodge, guides deer hunters in the fall, runs a trap line in the winter. He's also the best basket maker in the North Country. Sells 'em to the tourists in the summer. But there's some think the butter's run off Charlie's pancakes, so to speak. But don't you believe it."

Jason wrestled with what Bushy was telling them. *An Indian...who lives in caboose...and the butter's run off his pancakes?*

He was confused and now just a little scared. *Where are my parents taking me,* he wondered.

"What do you mean, the butter's run off his pancakes?" his father asked.

"Mostly, it's about the wolf."

This time Jason dropped the cider. "Are there...wolves up here?"

"Well, that depends on who you talk to," Bushy began. "The last wolf was killed in the Adirondacks a hundred years ago. But every once in a while someone claims to see one. What they think is a wolf is what we call a coydog—a cross between a coyote and a dog."

"Have you ever seen a real wolf?" Jason asked.

"Not around here," Bushy replied. "But Charlie Two Shirts— Whoa!" he called to the horses.

The sled came to a stop.

"There she is: the Wolf River."

Jason could hear the roar of the waterfall to his right.

"Oh, it's just beautiful," his mother exclaimed.

Jason turned back toward her. "Mom, what's it look like?"

"There's a ledge covered with blue ice," she began. "The water's cascading into a black, swirling pool at the bottom. The rocks in the river are capped with snow. They look like white mushrooms growing out of the water."

Jason could feel a cold mist drifting over his face. He heard his father clicking away with his camera.

"The river flows out of Algonquin Lake," Bushy said. "That's where the lodge sits."

"The lake is named after the Indians?" Jason's father asked.

"That's right," Bushy replied. "The Algonquins and Iroquois fought over this country for a century. The hunting was always good—plenty of moose and deer. Neither bunch ever had a permanent settlement. Winters were too rough. Charlie can tell you more. He's our resident expert, so to speak."

He snapped the reins. "Giddap, Jeb. Giddap, Joe."

The sled jerked ahead.

Jason tugged at Bushy's pant leg. "What about Charlie Two Shirts and the wolf?"

"Oh, you can ask Charlie about that yourself, Jason," Bushy replied. "He's looking forward to meeting you."

"Me?" Jason gushed. "How did he know I was coming?"

"Charlie's got a way of knowing things before other people know 'em. Know what I mean?"

Jason was trying to figure out what Bushy had just said when he heard a bird squawk.

"There's a blue jay!" he shouted.

"It's up ahead, sitting in an old white pine," Bushy replied. "Say, you've got quite an ear."

"When we took our hikes, Bill told me I heard more birds than he ever saw."

"What's a cardinal sound like?" Bushy asked. "We got a whole flock of 'em around the lodge."

28

"That's easy," Jason replied. "It's a whistle, like a cheer…cheer…cheer. Like that."

"Well, ain't that something?" Bushy boomed.

Another bird cawed above them.

"That's crow, up there," Jason shouted, pointing toward the limb of a lightning-scarred maple tree.

"You're close, partner," Bushy replied. "That's a raven. I don't expect you see—I mean have—any ravens back home."

Jason wiped his running nose with his glove. "A raven?" he asked. "It sure sounds like a crow."

"Well, almost," Bushy continued. "A raven looks like a crow, but it's twice as big. Charlie Two Shirts believes ravens are messengers of the Great Spirit. Says they have magical powers. If Charlie were here, he'd say that raven has a message for you."

"A message?" Jason's father gasped. "Give us a break."

"I don't understand," Jason muttered.

Bushy pulled back on the reins. "Charlie feels things, sees things other people don't."

Jeb and Joe came to an obedient stop.

"There's a boulder off to your right," he began. "To Charlie, that boulder is alive. And the raven and the blue jay you heard, they are his brothers and sisters."

"You're joking," his father laughed.

"Charlie calls it his medicine, his religion. It connects Charlie to what he calls the Great Mystery."

The raven called again, only louder, then flew off up the trail.

Bushy snapped the reins. "Giddap, Jeb. Giddap, Joe."

Chapter Three

Jason guessed they'd been on the trail for more than an hour. The horses' steaming breath drifted back into his face in an earthy mist. It was fun driving the bobsled, even if he couldn't see where he was going.

He wanted to know more about Charlie Two Shirts. What was the Great Mystery? And what did Bushy start to say about the wolves? Jason loved listening to the wolf cries on the CD's Bill had given him. He played them again and again. There was something in their eerie wail. He thought the wolves sounded lonely, kind of like him.

"There's the sign," his mother shouted, Wolf River Lodge." It was hanging from a cedar post at a fork in the trail. Its raised woodcut letters were painted gold with a black drop shadow. In the center of the sign was a large wolf's head carved from a thick slab of wood. The wolf was white with a touch of gray around its ears and nose.

Abbie gazed at the wolf. Its yellow eyes appeared to follow her as they passed.

"Bushy," she began, "you started to say something a ways back about this Charlie Two Shirts and a wolf. What did you mean?"

Todd nudged her knee. "I can't wait to hear this," he whispered.

But Jason was all ears. "Are there really...wolves?" he asked again.

"There were plenty of wolves around here in the old days," Bushy began. He looked at Jason. "But there was only one Spirit Wolf."

"A Spirit Wolf? What's...a Spirit Wolf?" Jason asked.

"For starters," Bushy continued, "the Spirit Wolf was a white wolf."

"A white wolf?" Jason asked.

"That's right, partner," Bushy said as he sipped his cider. "The legend goes back three hundred years. First, there was a Jesuit missionary—a Black Robe they called them. His name was John Paul Riche. He was living with the Algonquin Indians in Canada. The Mohawks—their territory was south of here—raided the village and took Riche prisoner. Treated him pretty rough. Even ripped out his fingernails so he couldn't untie the ropes around his hands."

"Ouch!" Jason cried.

"After the raid, the Mohawks headed south on Lake Champlain. Riche spent most of the trip tied up in the bottom of a canoe. Then the raiding party split up. Riche was taken southwest across the mountains.

"Somehow he managed to escape. But instead of backtracking to Lake Champlain, he headed west. Three days later, he ended up on the south shore of what we now call Algonquin Lake. He's sitting there on a rock, praying to God to help him find a way out of his mess, when a wolf howls in the woods in back of him. Well, Father Riche high-tails it down the beach. The poor man; he's probably half mad, what with all he's been through. He stops to catch his breath. That's when he sees it."

"The white wolf?" Jason asked.

"As white as the snow that's all around us," Bushy replied. "Riche runs for his life. Well, he must have fainted, because next thing he knows he's lying by a fire. There's a stranger sitting next to him. He's got Riche all bundled up in blankets, and he's cooking a stew.

"You've got to be kidding," Jason's mother gasped.

"Father Riche ended up back in France. Lived into his eighties. Always believed the white wolf and the stranger were one in the same—his guardian angel, so to speak."

Jason couldn't see his father roll his eyes.

"Sounds like a fairy tale to me," his father muttered.

But Jason was hooked. "Tell us another story about the white wolf," he urged Bushy.

"Next, there was a Scotsman named Ross," Bushy continued. "He was mapping this neck of the woods for the British. That was before the Revolutionary War. Ross was climbing Bald Bluff—that's on the other side of Algonquin Lake—when he took a terrible fall. Broke his leg. Cut his head, too. Bleeding pretty bad. Well, he just couldn't lie there, so he starts crawling off through the rocks, looking for a sheltered spot where he could try to patch himself up. He's just thankin' God he's alive. Then he heard it."

"The white wolf?" Jason asked.

"Ross looked up, and there it was," Bushy continued, "looking down on him from the top of the bluff. Ross tried to drag himself away, but just like Father Riche, he blacks out. Not surprising, losing all that blood. When he comes to, he's in a cave. A stranger's sitting with him around a small fire. Ross feels his leg. It's good as new, and the gash on his head is healed, too."

Todd's father was laughing. "Bushy, that's the best one yet."

"Oh, there's more to the story," Bushy continued. "The stranger Ross described sounds just like the fella that Father Riche wrote about, what, a hundred years before. Ross said he had long brown hair and a beard—and yellow eyes that glowed like they were on fire."

Jason's mother pulled the blankets up around her. "There can't be more...can there?"

"About a hundred years ago there was an Abnaki, an Indian by the name of Ethan Brown," Bushy replied.

"Here we go again," Jason's father laughed.

But Jason didn't think his father was funny. He loved listening to Bushy tell the white wolf stories. He wondered if they were really true. Bushy didn't sound like he was just making it all up.

"Ethan had a cabin up at Trout Pond," Bushy continued. "That's about three miles from the lodge, other side of the lake. Ethan and his daughter, Becky—just about your age, Jason—they were up the Wolf River a mile or so, picking blueberries. Ethan heard a rumbling out of the west. He figures there's a summer storm brewing. They better head for home. He and Becky jump in their canoe and paddle out onto the lake. When they round Buck Point, the wind hits 'em broadside. The canoe capsized, and Becky was swept under by the waves. Ethan swam to shore. It was a ten-mile hike back to his cabin, and it would be dark in a couple of hours. So he starts a fire to dry out best he could. Just sat there in the dark, crying his heart out. Oh, how he loved that little girl. He guessed it was about midnight when he heard it."

Jason suddenly realized the horses' reins had fallen from his hands. He'd forgotten all about Jeb and Joe.

"I got 'em," Bushy reassured him.

"Was it the white wolf again?" Jason asked.

"Well, it was a wolf. He knew that for sure," Bushy continued. "But it was dark. Ethan wished he'd had his rifle, but it was at the bottom of the lake. So he threw more wood on the fire. Sparks flyin' everywhere. That's when he saw it, plain as day."

"We know," Jason's father interrupted. "The white wolf!"

"It was white, that's for sure," Bushy continued, ignoring Jason's father. "It was the biggest wolf Ethan had ever seen, even back in Canada. Then the wolf walked out into the light, real slow. Circled Ethan a few times, then just sat back on its haunches and stared back at him from the other side of the fire. Ethan said he'd never forget the wolf's blazing yellow eyes, burning just like the flames from his campfire.

"Next thing Ethan knows, it's morning. The fire is just smoldering ashes. The white wolf has vanished, and the lake kind of disappeared, too, under a thick blanket of fog. The air was still as death, Ethan said later. Then he hears someone shouting, 'Hey, Pa!' *It can't be,* he thinks. It's his Becky!"

Jason heard his father kicking the bottom of the sled with his boot.

"What have you got in that cider?" his father asked.

"Oh, stop it, Todd," his mother said quickly. "This story is sort of, well, fascinating."

Jason pulled at Bushy's sleeve. "Did the white wolf bring Becky back?"

"Well, let me finish the story, partner," Bushy replied. "Then you can decide for yourself.

"Ethan ran down the beach toward the sound of Becky's voice. There's the canoe. There's Becky, floating toward him out of

36

the fog. There's a man paddling. They come ashore. Ethan said the man was about six feet tall, long brown hair and a beard, with yellow-green eyes that shimmered like emeralds. Ethan tried to speak, but he was tongue-tied. The stranger just nodded, put his hand on Ethan's shoulder, and smiled. Then he walked off down the beach and vanished into the mist. It was Ethan that first called the white wolf the Spirit Wolf. He said only the Great Spirit could have brought his Becky back."

Jason pulled at Bushy's sleeve again. "Did the Spirit Wolf...did it ever come back?"

"No one ever saw it again," Bushy replied. "But Charlie Two Shirts will tell you the Spirit Wolf never left, that it's out there right now, maybe on the other side of the ridge, maybe just behind that clump of cedar."

Jason smiled. But he didn't know what to believe. His parents were laughing in the back seat.

Maybe Bushy's just fooling...trying to make me feel good, he thought. *But Charlie Two Shirts is real, isn't he? Why does he believe the Spirit Wolf is real, and other people, like my parents, don't?*

Jason took another swipe at his running nose with the back of his glove. He was feeling cold again.

Abbie looked at Todd.

"Sounds like a pound of phony baloney to me," he said, shaking his head.

"I agree with you," she replied, "but...how could anyone make up a story so...unbelievable?"

There was a chirping sound from her husband's coat pocket. It was his cell phone.

Abbie sighed, her shoulders slumping beneath the blanket. Bushy shook his head, but he kept his thoughts to himself.

"Hello. Mike? I can barely hear you!" he shouted into the palm of his hand.

"Beam him up, Scotty," Bushy mumbled.

"I don't care what Sci-Tech is offering Children's Hospital," Todd growled, his connection temporarily restored. "Do whatever it takes to keep this account. Mike? Can you hear me? Mike? Damn, I lost him."

"Those cell phones don't work too well up here," Bushy chimed in. "They want to build a tower on Platt Peak, but there's plenty of opposition. Some say it'd be a real eyesore."

"Damn environmentalists," Todd grumbled.

"There's a phone in the lodge. No phones in your room, though," Bushy said.

"Can't Mike just handle it?" Abbie pleaded. "This is supposed to be our Christmas vacation."

"If I blow our biggest account, it's <u>hasta la vista</u>, baby," her husband fired back.

Bushy moved quickly to change the subject. "Gotta nice view coming up."

The sleigh broke out of a dense stand of white pine.

"There she is, right down there," Bushy said, pointing over the horses' heads. "Algonquin Lake. The lodge is off to the right."

"What's it look like, Mom? Tell me everything."

"We're on a ridge overlooking the lake," she began. "The sky is soft orange with traces of red. It's beginning to get dark. The snow is a mix of violet and gray, with splashes of white here and there. The lake is frozen, of course. The ice is a silvery blue. There's smoke curling up from two chimneys at the lodge. I can see a row of small cabins, too."

"I wonder which one is ours?" Jason asked.

"It looks like there's a small pond not too far from the lodge."

"That's Chapel Pond," Bushy said. "You can't see the chapel from this angle, though."

"There's a chapel?" Abbie asked.

"Sure is, Mrs. Quinn," Bushy replied. "Built by Pierre LaFontaine himself. He built the lodge. Charlie Two Shirts lives in back."

"In his caboose, right?" Todd quipped.

Bushy guided the sleigh down off the ridge. They crossed Wolf River again. Jason listened as the river churned and tumbled beneath him. The horses clip-clopped over a narrow wood bridge. Joe let loose with a loud snort.

"That old horse can taste his oats from here, by golly," Bushy chuckled.

"We must be close," Jason said. "I can smell smoke."

He wiggled on the hard seat. He'd be glad to sit by a warm fire. He wondered how long it would take him to learn his way around the cabin. And the lodge—what would that be like? He was thinking about his parents, too, but mostly his father. He could tell his father wasn't having a good time.

Abbie gazed wide-eyed from beneath her blankets. The lodge was just ahead. The trail was lined with snow-capped pine trees, which rose about sixty feet into the raw winter sky.

"Those trees," she stammered.

"We call them old growth pines," Bushy replied. "This area's never been logged, thank goodness."

"Everything looks so perfect," Abbie gushed. "Better than I ever imagined."

Her smile disappeared when she looked at her husband. But she put her arm around him and gave him a kiss on the cheek.

Todd looked as skeptical as ever. He squinted disapprovingly at the sight of an old, battered green pickup truck, spotting its crumpled nose poking out from between stacks of split firewood piled in a sagging shed by the edge of the trail. A bright orange electric cord dangled from a cracked socket nailed to a 2x4 rafter. The cord snaked its way down from the ceiling and under the truck's dented hood.

"That truck still run?" he asked.

"She's a tired old gal," Bushy replied, "but she's still got enough left to haul firewood and garbage around the place."

"What's the electric cord all about?" Todd continued.

"There's a sixty-watt bulb at the other end. Keeps the oil from turning to sludge when she drops below zero, which is most every night this time of year."

Bushy brought the sleigh to a stop in front of an immense stone stairway.

"Welcome to Wolf River Lodge," he announced.

Inside, someone was playing **White Christmas** on a piano badly in need of a tuning. Bushy jumped down and tied Jeb and Joe to a worn hitching post. He lifted Jason gently to the ground.

"Here you are, partner."

Todd leapt from the back seat. "Hey, Bushy. Where's that phone?"

"Just inside. Take a left down the hall."

Todd disappeared into the lodge.

Jason took his mother's elbow. They started up the steps.

"What's the lodge look like, Mom?"

"It's bigger than I expected," she began. "The outside is all bark. There's a porch across the front. The roof is supported with pillars that look like giant trees."

"They're cedar," Bushy explained. "Those are spruce slabs on the exterior walls. The windows are trimmed in split yellow birch. The roof's corrugated sheet metal. The snow slides off, most of the time. When it doesn't, we have to climb up there and shovel it off. Go in and register. I'll get your gear unloaded. Meet you right here."

Jason followed his mother inside. The door thundered shut behind him. He turned his head from side to side, trying to get the feel of the room.

Where are the walls? The piano. That's easy. It's off to the right. Must be another room. The kitchen's close. I can smell spaghetti sauce.

"What's that hissing sound?" he asked.

"Those must be gas lamps," his mother answered. "We're in the lobby. The walls are knotty pine. There are some old photographs on the wall, women in long white dresses, men with straw hats, paintings of deer, hunters in canoes. Oh, Jason, there's a black bear with a red bandana tied around its neck. It's standing in the corner!"

"A real…bear?" Jason asked.

"Don't worry," she replied. "It's stuffed—I hope. The dining room is off to the left," she continued. "They're setting tables for dinner. The living room is off to the right. There's a huge Christmas tree, Jason. It must be fifteen feet tall."

"Who's singing **Jingle Bells**?" he asked.

"Five or six people. They're standing around an upright piano, like the one your grandmother has. Oh, Jason, there's a moose head hanging over the biggest stone fireplace I've ever seen. And all these hats are hanging from its antlers."

Jason laughed. "Where's the TV coming from?"

His mother looked around. "There's a bar off the living room. Some men are watching a football game."

Now that Jason had a sense of things, he tried to visualize each room. Every sound, every smell helped paint a picture. He stood quietly in the middle of the lobby, taking everything in.

Abbie noticed an attractive woman get up from a small roll-top desk and walk briskly toward them. She was lean and long-limbed. She skimmed over the floor, as if she were on cross-country skis.

"You must be the rest of the Quinn family," she said. "I met your husband on his way to the phone. I'm Kate Boone. Welcome to Wolf River Lodge."

She looked to be in her mid-forties. Her grayish-blonde hair was cut short. She had lively brown eyes and a wide smile.

"You're in Porcupine," Mrs. Quinn. "It's the first cabin on the river trail. Bushy will show you the way, help you get settled."

Abbie filled out the registration form. She couldn't see Todd, but she could hear him shouting into the phone. So could Jason.

"Mrs. Boone, is that spaghetti sauce I smell?" Jason asked.

"That's right, and wait till you taste it. We've got the best sauce in the North Country. Dinner is served from six to seven," she added. "I'll see you then and fill you in on our Christmas program." She rushed back to her desk to answer the phone.

Todd caught up to them near the front door.

"Was getting to the phone that important?" Abbie asked.

"It comes with the territory," he shot back. "If I don't make the numbers this quarter—"

43

"I know," she sighed. "It's hasta la vista, baby."

Bushy was waiting at the foot of the stairs. He had their luggage piled in a weather-beaten wood wheelbarrow.

"Follow me," he said, pushing off down a narrow trail that wound its way through the woods in back of the lodge.

The temperature was dropping as fast as the sun. The fading light brushed a crimson purple glaze over the fresh-fallen snow.

"What's that humming noise?" Jason asked.

"Surprised you can hear it," Bushy replied. "That's our generator. Noah Boone went to a lot of trouble to soundproof the shed. That's where we get our electricity."

The trail dipped through a mix of snow-draped hemlock and yellow birch trees.

Jason pulled at his mother's arm. "Are we there yet?"

Before she could answer, Bushy called back to them, "This is it. Watch your step; there's a little ice on the deck."

His mother told him the cabin was bark, just like the lodge, and that there was a neat pile of firewood, right by the door. Jason could hear the river clearly.

"Let's get your things inside," Bushy huffed.

He tucked a duffel bag under each of his blacksmith arms, climbed the steps, pushed open the door with his foot, and flipped on the light switch.

"Home, sweet home," he bellowed.

Jason followed his mother inside.

"Oh, how lovely," she exclaimed.

Jason stood quietly at her side. It smelled like wood smoke. He could already tell it was small, just by listening to Bushy move around.

"Let's take a tour, Jason," his mother said. "We're standing in a small kitchen. Over the sink there's a window that looks out on the river. There's a small refrigerator, a stove, and a place to hang our coats. Oh, what's this?"

"What, Mom?'

"There's a long sheet of paper thumb-tacked to the wall."

"What's it say?"

She looked at it quickly.

Please Read Carefully
1. **Don't waste our delicious spring water.**
2. **All plants and animals are protected.**
3. **No alcoholic beverages or bottles on dock.**
4. **Use fireplace carefully.**
5. **Don't even think of feeding the bears.**

"It says we better not feed the bears," she replied. "Thank God they're hibernating. Let's go in the living room. It's just off to the left. Here's your cane. You should try to use it."

Jason held his mother's elbow with his left hand while sweeping his cane with his right.

"The walls are paneled with rough-cut cedar boards," she began.

But Jason stopped suddenly. "What's that?" he asked, poking his cane at his feet.

"Oh, it looks like a grate of some kind. That must be where the heat comes from the furnace." She continued their tour. "We're standing in the middle of the living room. Straight ahead—here, follow me—there's a large, high-backed couch in front of a beautiful stone fireplace."

"It's pure Adirondack granite," Bushy said.

Jason had heard the door shut. He assumed Bushy and his father were carrying in more bags.

"LaFontaine cut and fit every stone himself," Bushy said.

"Anything around here LaFontaine didn't do?" his father asked.

Jason continued his tour. He walked slowly, barely lifting his feet. He wanted to get the feel of the floor, where it dipped toward the back of the cabin, where the rug ended and the linoleum in the kitchen began.

"There's a small coffee table here in front of the couch," his mother continued. "There's a floor lamp on the right side."

Jason reached out with his cane. He ran his hand over the back of the couch.

"There are two stuffed chairs to the left of the couch," his mother continued, "with a lamp in between."

He walked over and touched the chairs. He felt the shape and texture of as much as he could. These landmarks—with practice— would enable him to move about the cabin by himself.

"Let's go down the hall to the bathroom and bedrooms," his mother suggested. "We'll begin here by the couch. Try it."

Jason took five small steps.

Great, he thought. *Now turn left, and walk down the hallway.*

"You're doing just fine," his mother said.

He kept walking, feeling the wall with the back of his hand. He stopped when he felt a doorway on his left.

"That's your bedroom," his mother told him.

She showed him where the bed and dresser were. Then they walked to the bathroom at the end of the hall. His mother began to laugh.

"What's so funny, Mom?"

"There's a card taped to the mirror. It says, 'Please don't clean your snowmobiles with our bathroom linen. We have cloths for you in the lobby.' "

After Jason learned his way around the bathroom, he located his parents' bedroom across the hall, then walked on his own back into the living room.

"Why don't you rest on the couch for a minute while your father and I put things away," his mother suggested. "Then you can practice getting around on your own."

Jason felt for the edge of couch. When he found it, he collapsed into a pile of pine-scented pillows. He'd never felt so tired.

Todd tossed the last of their bags on the floor.

"There's a few things you'll need to know," Bushy began. "This isn't like home. When the generator shuts down, about ten every night, your lights run on batteries. Make sure you turn 'em off before you go to bed. We use propane for heat. It's a real chore hauling it in, so keep the thermostat at sixty-eight—no higher, please. With the fireplace, you'll be just fine. There's plenty of firewood on the deck. You'll find kindling and newspapers in the wood box."

He looked at Todd with a raised eyebrow.

"Know how to start a fire and keep it going, Mr. Quinn?"

"I was an Eagle Scout," Todd replied, folding his arms impatiently.

"Good," Bushy answered. "Two logs on the bottom, one on top will do just fine. Anything more, heat just goes up the chimney."

He walked to the picture window. "Here's our featured attraction."

He flipped a light switch.

"This is your floodlight. There's a red metal can on the deck. It's filled with corn. We feed a sizeable deer herd all winter. I'll sprinkle some outside when I leave. I guarantee you'll have half a dozen deer or more here in no time. That's about it. Any questions?"

Todd shook his head.

Bushy headed for the door.

"If you need anything, just give a holler."

"Oh, Todd, isn't this place incredible?" Abbie exclaimed.

"I've been here long enough," he replied. "Where's my drink?" He headed for the kitchen. "The bar is open."

48

He found two glasses and filled them with ice. He treated himself to a generous four-fingers pour. Abbie got a single shot. He filled the rest of her glass with water.

When he walked back into the living room, Jason was standing in front of the couch with his cane.

"Give it a try, Jason," he said as he tipped his glass back and took a long swallow. The whiskey burned as it rolled down his throat.

"Why does this stuff taste so good?" he asked under his breath.

Jason turned to his left and took six cautious steps, all the while sweeping his cane in front of him. Click.

Click.

Something in front of me, better stop, he thought. *What is it?* He reached out with his right hand. *Feels like the chair. OK. I went too far. Better take two steps back. There's the edge of the couch. So if I turn left, take maybe two steps ahead, turn left again, and walk straight ahead, I should be close to the bathroom.*

But he slipped on a loose throw rug and crashed to the floor.

"Jason, are you all right?" his mother cried. She rushed to his side.

"Leave him alone, Abbie," his father said. "He's got to learn from his mistakes."

Jason got back up on his own and continued his journey. The trick was to remember how long it took to walk from one place to the next. It was impossible to keep track of how many steps it took.

Todd stared into his glass, twirled the ice cubes, and took another deep drink.

"How am I doing now?" Jason called from the hallway.

"Right on target," Todd replied. "The bathroom's straight ahead."

Jason walked in and closed the door.

Abbie took her drink and sank down on the couch. The fire crackled at her feet.

"Well, it's been quite a day," she sighed. "I'm whipped."

Todd gave her a kiss on the cheek.

"Welcome to Fort Wilderness."

Chapter Four

"It's pretty quiet in there," Jason said. "Are you guys okay?"

He was feeling his way along the back hall. He thought he had a pretty good idea of what the living room looked like.

Just don't bust anything, he kept telling himself. *And don't fall again.*

He wondered if his parents were in one of their moods. He could tell when they were feeling sorry for him—or themselves. And that didn't make things any easier. He still had his bad days, more than they would ever know. A couple of times he even thought about taking a bunch of pills. He knew what the aspirin bottle felt like, how the pills rattled in the little plastic container, how to push and turn the round cap. His parents still loved him; that wasn't the problem. He was the problem. At least that's how he felt sometimes. Maybe, as he learned to take care of himself, his parents could have their lives back. His mother had given up her job at the nursery school. She didn't even go to lunch with her friends much anymore.

There's the edge of the wall, he thought. *The couch should be just a few steps ahead and to my right.*

Jason could hear his father twirling the ice cubes in his drink. His father hadn't been the same since the accident. They used to have a lot of fun together.

Dad's trying, but sometimes he just forgets I'm blind. And then he gets mad.

Jason reached out with his right hand.

That's it, the back of the couch.

He settled into the couch and let the warmth from the fireplace wash over him.

"We're still here," his mother replied with a laugh that was labored and limp.

Abbie was staring out the picture window, lost in the snow that swirled in the floodlight like sparks from a campfire.

"I wish Jason could see this," she cried softly to herself.

Several deer had already discovered the corn Bushy had scattered beneath the window. Their thick nutmeg coats seemed to glow under the bright light. Occasionally, one would raise its head, twitch its ears, and then quickly return to its free meal. Abbie frowned when one stood on its hind legs and shoved the smallest away from the feast.

She looked at the small deer and then at Jason. She wondered if the doctors were being honest with them, or just trying to bolster their spirits. Could any sort of healing occur? Was there any real chance her son would ever see…anything again?

Jason was handling it remarkably well, learning to live all over again. She wished she could say the same for Todd. He looked at her with a kind of sardonic weariness, then slipped back into his morose trance in front of the fire.

His infinite optimism, self-confidence, and wry sense of humor—the qualities that attracted her to him when they met eleven years ago—were now overshadowed by increasingly dark spells of self-pity and cynicism. He wore the pain of the past eight months like a horribly wrinkled suit. Once a muscular, robust man with thick, jet-black hair, he seemed to be shrinking, growing gaunt and gray before her eyes.

Todd took a long sip from his drink. He looked at his watch. Maybe he had time for one more…one for the trail, so to speak. He gazed into the fire.

What a way to celebrate Christmas, he thought. *What's it supposed to be about, the birth of the Son of God? If there is a God, where was he when Jason fell? Watching over the Catholics?*

Todd knew his church attendance was sporadic at best. He mumbled his way through the hymns and prayers. And now the thought that Jason's accident was some sort of Almighty payback for his own impiety was beginning to haunt him.

Abbie, of course, had a different take. She and Jason attended church almost every Sunday. She'd told Todd more than once that God didn't cause Jason's blindness, and neither did he. Still, he couldn't kick his guilt trip.

Perhaps his life, until now, had simply been too easy. He grew up on Rochester's affluent eastside, lettered in four sports, and graduated in the top ten percent of his class. His parents footed the whole bill at the University of Rochester. He just worked for beer money.

His good luck continued after graduation. He interviewed on campus with America's largest medical equipment company and was hired almost immediately. In eleven years, he worked his way up the pyramid to eastern regional sales manager. *Ain't life grand,* he often thought.

Until Jason's accident.

And now here they were, thanks to Abbie and her big ideas. He had to admit the scenery was spectacular. He hadn't been in the Adirondacks since his Boy Scout days at Camp Massawepie. Wolf River Lodge was stunning. Even their little cabin had an unvarnished charm about it. But he couldn't figure where Bushy was coming from. Oh, he was an authentic character, but there was something about the man that had Todd stumped. He wasn't your run of the mill woodchuck; Todd knew that right away. There was more to the man, more to this whole place than met the eye.

Well, we're here, he decided. *Might as well make the best of it.* He threw back his drink, tossed the ice cubes into the fire, and joined Abbie at the window. He pointed to a large deer that now had most of the corn to itself.

"I'll bet that's a buck. They lose their horns about now."

He walked back to the couch.

"Jason, what do you think so far?"

"Driving the bobsled was pretty neat," he replied. "And I liked the story about the white wolf, too."

Todd slammed his empty glass down on the table.

"I don't know about the rest of you, but I'm starved. Let's eat."

Abbie got their coats. Todd poked at the burning logs and checked the fireplace screen. He hoped the cabin wouldn't burn to the ground while they were eating dinner.

They walked out onto the porch. There was a loud snort.

"What was that?" Jason asked.

"It was a deer," his father answered.

"Oh, Jason, I wish you could see them," Abbie blurted out. She put her hand on her mouth and closed her eyes.

Todd bit down on his lip. He gave Jason a hug. "Take my arm."

The trail back to the lodge was easy to follow, even in the dark. But Todd flipped on his flashlight, just to be on the safe side.

The dining room was about half full. Maybe a dozen people were scattered about the room. The tables were draped with green and red tablecloths. A Christmas wreath hung over a large stone fireplace. The logs crackled and popped on the raised hearth.

"I wonder if we just sit down or what?" Abbie asked.

"Here comes someone who looks like he's in charge," Todd replied.

"Welcome to Wolf River lodge. I'm Noah Boone. It's nice to have you with us."

Todd winced as the square-shouldered innkeeper squeezed down on his hand. *This mountain man handshake must be some kind of ritual,* he thought. Todd decided to squeeze back, but Noah Boone clearly had the advantage.

Todd guessed Noah to be in his late sixties or early seventies. He was a lean yet muscular man, chisel-faced and mostly bald, but for small patches of curly gray hair bunched around his ears. He had wooly black eyebrows that arched over his steely-blue eyes. His smile was wide and just a bit mischievous. He was the kind of man, Todd thought, who could fill a room by himself.

Noah knelt down and put his callused hand on Jason's shoulder.

"Bushy tells me you know the song of every bird in the woods. Is that true, Jason?"

"I like nature a lot, Mr. Boone," Jason replied. "It's fun listening to birds and stuff."

"Well, we've got plenty of wild stuff up here," Noah said with a chuckle.

"Are there wolves up here?" Jason asked. "Bushy told us about the white wolf. He said Charlie...Two Shirts said it was real."

"I think we've heard enough about this so-called Spirit Wolf for one day," Todd said quickly.

"Mr. Boone, are ravens...messengers?" Jason continued. "Bushy said a raven talked to me today."

Noah stood and tousled Jason's hair.

"When you come to the mountains," he replied, "you may find more than you seek."

Todd looked at Abbie with a raised eyebrow. *Here we go again,* he thought.

Noah showed them to a table near the fireplace.

"Our daughter, Jody, will be your server. She's home from college, helping out over the holidays."

Abbie looked nervously around the room. People were watching them. Some were whispering.

A willowy, apple-cheeked girl with short auburn hair approached their table.

"Hi, my name is Jody. Welcome to Wolf River Lodge."

"Your dad said you're home from college?" Abbie asked.

"I'm at Paul Smiths. I didn't stray far from home."

"You grew up here...at the lodge?" Todd asked.

"Sure did," she answered with a smile.

"It must be fifty miles to the nearest school," Abbie said.

"That's about right. I went to school in Old Forge."

"If you can't drive in or out of here, how did you get there?" Todd asked.

"I met the school bus at Wolf River Station, where you left your car."

"How did you get to the station?" Abbie asked. "In the bobsled?"

"Dad took me in the truck. We drove it on the old railroad tracks. In the winter we rode one of the snowmobiles."

Abbie shook her head. "I can't imagine it."

"Sounds like fun," Jason said.

Everyone laughed. Jody reviewed the featured entrees.

"Can I bring you something from the bar to get you started?"

Abbie ordered a glass of Chablis, Todd his usual CC on the rocks. Jason asked for a Coke.

Noah and Kate Boone were rearranging tables nearby for a large group.

"Please stop by the desk after dinner," Kate said. "I want to tell you what's planned for tomorrow and Christmas Day."

Jody returned with their drinks.

"May I take your order?"

"Jason will have the spaghetti and meatballs," Abbie began. "I'd like the chicken parm."

Todd ordered a strip steak.

"How would you like that cooked?" Jody asked.

"Pittsburgh," he replied.

"Pittsburgh?"

"Burned on the outside," he replied, "raw in the center."

Abbie helped Jason find his Coke. It was in a tall plastic cup. He took a long sip through his straw.

"Jody, is Charlie Two Shirts here tonight?" he asked.

"He stopped by the kitchen earlier. Picked up a chicken dinner and took it back to his place. You'll probably see him in the morning."

Jody's face flushed with her awkward choice of words. She rushed away toward the kitchen.

"Do you know about the white wolf?" Jason asked.

"She's gone," Abbie answered. "She…went to get our salads."

He grabbed for his cup but knocked it over instead. Ice cubes and Coke cascaded across the tablecloth and poured onto the floor.

He heard chair legs screeching across the old wood floor as his parents jumped to their feet. He could feel the cold Coke dripping off the table and onto his lap. *You jerk,* he said to himself.

"I'm sorry, you guys. I just don't like it when people walk away without telling me, that's all."

"She…she just didn't know," his mother replied.

She tried to dry Jason's lap the best she could with her napkin.

"I'll get a towel," Todd said.

He rushed out of the dining room and into the bar. He had to squeeze past a fleshy, swag-bellied man seated on a stool near the doorway.

"Excuse me."

"No problem, pal," the man replied. A pudgy teenage boy and a blonde, bushy-haired woman who reminded Todd of Phyllis Diller were seated next to him. Todd assumed they were the man's wife and son.

Two men wearing insulated overalls were engaged in a heated game of 8-ball. The bartender was nowhere in sight. Todd found a towel and headed for the door.

"Hey, pal. The kid—is he blind or what?"

"Yes, he is," Todd answered, clenching his teeth.

"Too bad. Hey, let me buy you a drink," the man replied.

"No thanks," Todd said coldly before hurrying back to the dining room.

Abbie was still wiping up the mess. Kate Boone had pitched in with another towel and fresh table settings. Jody wasn't far behind with their salads, a basket of fresh baked rolls, and another Coke.

"Jody," Jason said, picking up where he left off, "do you know about the white wolf?"

"The Spirit Wolf? Oh, yes," Jody replied. "When I was a little girl, Charlie Two Shirts told me so many wonderful stories. He made me this necklace. He said the Spirit Wolf would always protect me."

She pulled a silver chain from behind her red apron.

"See? Oh, I'm sorry," she said, once again realizing her mistake. She hurried off to another table.

"She's gone again," Jason said, "isn't she?"

His mother gave him a hug.

"She didn't mean anything, Jason. She just isn't used to being around someone who is blind."

Jason found his Coke this time without incident. He took a deep sip.

"What did the necklace look like?" he asked.

"It looked like a wolf's head, about the size of a quarter," his mother replied. "It might have been carved from a piece of bone."

Todd was laughing.

"What's so funny?" Abbie asked.

"It sounds to me like this Charlie Two Shirts may have his bow strung backwards," Todd quipped. "They probably keep this guy around just to entertain the tourists."

Jody returned ten minutes later with their meals. She'd regained her composure.

"Save room for dessert," she advised. "We've got apple pie and homemade ice cream."

The obnoxious man Todd confronted in the bar was ambling across the dining room. He had a pitcher of beer in one hand, a full pint in the other. He stopped at several tables. He seemed to know everyone in the dining room. The blonde-haired woman and the lumpish boy followed along silently. Jody was clearing an adjacent table. Todd caught her attention.

"Say, Jody, who is that guy?"

"Big Tony? That's Tony Delmonte."

"He acts like he's running for mayor," Todd said.

"Big Tony comes up to snowmobile four, maybe five times every winter," Jody replied. "That's his wife, Tina, and son, Joey. Big Tony's talking to Liz Blackstone. She has 20,000 acres near the west end of the lake."

"Twenty thousand acres?" Todd exclaimed.

"Her father was one of William Seward Webb's partners. Webb built the railroad through here."

"Bushy told us about him," Todd nodded.

"Liz is getting up in years," Jody continued. "She'll be eighty-five in June. She has no heirs. The state wants to buy her land. The purchase is key to a proposed new wilderness area. The trouble is, Big Tony is after it, too. He's a developer in New Jersey. He wants to build luxury vacation homes here. It's all part of an exclusive resort he's promoting. He calls it the Osprey Club."

She waved her towel toward the lake.

"If he buys it, everything here will change, and not for the better."

The apple pie exceeded Jody's promise. The crust was thick and crisp, the apples tart and juicy. Abbie suggested they finish their coffee in the living room, where Noah Boone was laying fresh logs on the fire.

"That fireplace is spectacular," Todd remarked.

"There isn't a tool mark on it anywhere," Noah replied. "A real tribute to Pierre's craftsmanship."

Todd ran his hand over the massive stone mantel. "How long did it take him to build this place?"

"About a year," Noah replied. "Never had a blueprint or formal plan. Just sketched what he dreamed up on scraps of paper. The beams are peeled spruce logs. The walls are paneled in birch that's been rubbed with linseed oil. Gives it a nice, warm tint."

Kate Boone joined them at the Christmas tree.

"Getting the grand tour?" she asked.

"I've got to check on the generator," her husband said, excusing himself. "I'll see you in the morning."

"And it's going to be a beautiful morning," Kate replied. "Bright sunshine and the temperature in the high twenties. They're calling for heavy snow and wind gusts up to thirty miles an hour by late afternoon, so I encourage you to get outdoors early. Breakfast is served from seven to eight-thirty, lunch from noon to one-thirty. We have ten miles of cross-country ski trails and ski rentals if you didn't bring your own."

"Are the trails flat?" Abbie asked. "Jason hasn't used his skis since the accident. He wants to try it."

"I'll be okay," Jason said quickly.

"I'd suggest the Pond Loop Trail," Kate said, adding, "there's a Christmas Eve service at the chapel tomorrow night. It begins around six, or when Father Mulcahy gets here. Father Mike rides up from Old Forge on his snowmobile. He has dinner with us afterwards, then rides back to conduct an eleven o'clock service at his own church."

Todd shook his head.

"He's been doing it for years. It's a, well, non-denominational service. Father Mike is sort of a free spirit."

"What exactly do you mean?" Abbie asked.

"He's a great guy; don't get me wrong. But he's in hot holy water with the Catholic Church. The Vatican doesn't share his views on women, gays—that sort of thing."

"Like what with women?" Abbie continued.

"For starters, Father Mike encourages women to assist him in his services, say the homily, for instance. He also permits non-Catholics to take communion in his church. Things are getting pretty tense with his bishop. Father Mike may break away and establish a congregation. People up here just love him."

She took a sip from her coffee.

"We welcome our guests to open gifts with us at nine on Christmas morning. It's an old Wolf River Lodge tradition. A turkey dinner with all the trimmings is served at noon. Any questions?"

Abbie took Jason's hand.

"Sounds great. What do you think?"

"This place is kinda cool," Jason said, stifling a long yawn.

"Well, it's cool right now, that's for sure," Kate said.

"It's been a long day," Todd said. "Let's head for home—the cabin, that is."

As they left the lodge, Todd noticed the man called Big Tony was back in the bar, holding court with three other men. *What a perfect ass,* he thought to himself. He hoped he could avoid the man for the rest of their stay.

Abbie suggested they walk down to the edge of the lake. She'd never seen the stars so bright. They shimmered like bits of crystal in the cold, ink-black sky.

"I hope there's something left in the fireplace," she said while briskly rubbing her hands. Her breath rose into the air like chimney smoke from the lodge.

Jason stood next to his father, poking at the snow with his boot.

"Dad, do you think the Spirit Wolf was real?"

"Jason, don't believe a word of it," his father replied.

"Oh, Todd," Abbie protested.

"Trust me, Jason. It's pure bull. And don't get all fired up about this Charlie Two Shirts. An Indian who lives in a caboose and talks to the wolves—jeez!"

A fireball raged across the sky over the lake.

"Look," his mother shouted, "a shooting star!"

Jason blinked. He blinked again. *Did I see it, or did I just think I saw it,* he wondered.

Pictures sometimes flashed in his eyes, only to vanish as quickly. He'd been warned it might happen. Doctor Kerr said his memory might play tricks on him. When he dreamed, everything was so real, just like he could see again. But now he felt dizzy, as if the rolling thunderbolt had spun him in circles as it streaked overhead. He grabbed his father's coat sleeve.

"What's the matter, Jason?" his father asked.

"I don't know. I feel kind of weak."

Abbie took off a glove and felt his forehead.

"He's burning up. I hope you're not coming down with a bug or something," she said.

All that was left in the fireplace were smoldering embers. While Abbie helped Jason off to bed, Todd found the kindling and soon had the fire crackling again. She joined him on the couch.

"Quite a day, wouldn't you say?"

"How's Jason doing?" Todd asked.

He's got a fever, that's for sure. Maybe he's getting a cold. I know he needs a good night's sleep."

Todd squeezed his wife's knee. "Let's just sleep here tonight," he joked.

She laid her head on his shoulder. They both stared into the flames that jumped across the burning logs like dancers on a sizzling stage.

"Jason's getting a little carried away with this wolf business," Todd began. "A couple of times, I thought about asking Barnes to can it. I don't like him—or any of these yokels—filling Jason's head with a lot of nonsense."

"Oh, Todd, if it gives him a sense of excitement and adventure, what the heck?"

He kissed her softly on the cheek. "Speaking of excitement."

He flipped off the light.

Chapter Five

Cr-r-ruck. Cr-r-ruck. Cr-r-ruck.

Jason rubbed the sleep from his eyes. The sun was streaming through his bedroom window. Its comforting glow rolled over his face like a soft, warm towel.

It must be morning, he thought.

Cr-r-ruck. Cr-r-ruck.

It was a raven. He guessed it was perched right outside his window. He wondered if it was the messenger—the same raven that Bushy said called to him yesterday.

He climbed from bed. The icy cabin floor was a shocking reminder he wasn't at home. And so was the dresser he stumbled into before finding the door. At home, he was becoming increasingly self-sufficient. But the cabin was uncharted territory; moving from one room to the next was like a sighted person walking through a furniture store blindfolded. He made his way down the hall to the bathroom.

His father was waiting for him. "I'll give you a hand with the shower. It's a little different than home."

The warm water felt good in the cold, drafty bathroom.

Afterward, he dressed himself. He found his wool pants by feel. That was easy. He wanted to wear his red turtleneck under his favorite blue sweater. So he felt for the button. His mother had sewn a small plastic button on the inside near the waist. The blue turtleneck had two buttons. The blue sweater was next. It had a small square piece of cloth sewn in the same place as the turtleneck. His brown sweater had a round piece of cloth. The socks were easy, too; they were wool, and all white.

They left the cabin for breakfast just after eight. The trail to the lodge was freshly plowed. The sky was sapphire blue. Snow hung from the trees like dollops of thick whipped cream. At first, Jason struggled to breathe in the icy morning air.

Cr-r-ruck. Cr-r-ruck.

"I wonder if the raven is following us," Jason said.

"Following us?" his mother asked.

"It was outside my bedroom window this morning," Jason replied. "Maybe it's the messenger."

"Here we go again," his father mumbled.

70

"Maybe it's just wishing you a merry Christmas," his mother said quickly.

The raven kept pace, flying from one tree to the next. When they reached the lodge, it called out again and flew off across the lake.

Good riddance, his father thought. *I hope that's the last we see of the damned bird.*

The dining room was nearly full. There was a short line moving along a breakfast buffet that was set up by the front window. Todd noticed Big Tony Delmonte right away. He was standing near the fireplace, talking with two men Todd hadn't seen the night before.

Noah Boone met them at the doorway.

"Good morning. And how are all the Quinns this fine Christmas Eve morning?"

Abbie was struck by the liveliness in his eyes. His smile was warm, yet there was an authoritarian air about him. He was ruggedly handsome—almost sexy, she thought, for a man who must be in his early seventies.

There must be something in the mountain air, she supposed, *or maybe it's his young wife. She's got to be twenty years younger than him.*

"Have a seat anywhere," he continued. "I recommend the blueberry pancakes topped with pure Adirondack maple syrup—from our own sugar shack, I might add."

"Sounds delicious," Abbie said.

71

"Stop by the office after breakfast. Pick up a trail map. The cross-country skiing couldn't be better."

"Mom, can we sit by the fire?" Jason asked.

"How are you feeling?" Abbie asked. "You had a bit of a fever last night. In the rush, I forgot to check this morning."

"I'm fine," he replied.

But, in fact, he felt chilled. And he was still a little woozy from last night, when they saw the shooting star, when he thought he saw...something. He'd woken up with a headache, too. He decided to keep quiet. He didn't want to alarm them.

There was one cleared table near the fireplace. Big Tony and the men he'd been talking with were now seated nearby. Big Tony's back was turned.

Thank goodness, Todd thought. He didn't want to have to talk to the jerk.

Jason sat quietly at the table while his parents went through the buffet line. He couldn't help overhear the conversation at Big Tony's table.

"Duff, a piece of property like this comes along once in a hundred years," a gravely-voiced man said. Jason guessed it was the man they called Big Tony. He remembered his voice from the dining room last night. "Twenty-four million is a bargain. Fifty exclusive investors, a hundred-and-fifty thousand each. Financing for the rest is just about lined up. We'll build one hundred luxury vacation homes, priced from $450,000 to just under a million. There's more in the prospectus. Here, take a look."

"Now wait a minute, Tony," another man began. "Who in their right mind would pay that kind of money for a place that doesn't even have road access? And besides, the Adirondack Park Agency's not going to let you waltz in here and turn this place into Lake George."

"Duff, that's what most people think," Big Tony replied. "Part one: There's a 5,000-acre parcel between the Blackstone estate and the Kulpsford Road. I hope to close on it next week. Its owner is throwing in with us."

"Interesting," Jason heard another man say.

Part two:" Big Tony continued, "The old New York Central line runs through the lower corner of Liz Blackstone's place. You know they want to open that line again, from Utica all the way to Lake Placid. I'm working with friends in Washington and Albany to help secure funding for the railroad's developers. The kind of buyers we're targeting will stand in line to vacation like the Vanderbilts and the Rockefellers did a century ago…ride in our own Pullman car, from Grand Central Station in Manhattan to their private camp at the Osprey Club, the Adirondacks' most exclusive address."

Jason heard the rustle of papers.

"Here's a sketch of the railroad depot we'll build—for Osprey members only, of course."

"Jason, I hope you're hungry," his father said. "These are lumberjack-sized pancakes. Jason?"

"Oh, sorry, Dad. I was listening to those men over there." He pointed to the table where Big Tony was making his sales pitch.

"Jason, you know it's not polite to listen in on other people's conversations," his mother said.

He gave her a sheepish grin.

"Dad, is the lake for sale? That's what they were talking about. You know—what Jody said last night."

"I guess you know more about it than I do," his father replied. "Let's dig into these pancakes."

As Abbie got Jason started, Todd watched Big Tony walk to another nearby table. He spread out what looked like blueprints. His conversation became animated. Todd couldn't hear what he was saying.

"I think my eyes were bigger than my stomach," Abbie laughed. She stared down at a heaping stack of pancakes surrounded by scrambled eggs and sausage links.

"How's breakfast so far?" Kate Boone asked, stopping at their table. "I brought you a fresh pot of coffee."

"There'll be no leftovers at this table, I guarantee it," Todd boasted.

He wiped some maple syrup from his chin. Jason was doing the same.

"Kate, uh, Big Tony—I guess that's what they call him—Jody was telling us he's trying to put together some big land deal up here."

74

Kate poured herself a cup of coffee. She glanced quickly around the dining room, then sat down.

"Well, there's more to it than that," she began. "Liz Blackstone is going to sell; that's not the issue. It's to whom."

"We saw Big Tony talking to her last night," Abbie said.

"Liz's husband, Wilcox, passed away ten years ago," Kate continued. "She's been waiting almost three years for the state to make her an offer. I think her patience is wearing a little thin. Big Tony is trying to put a deal together that, as they say, she can't refuse."

"He said twenty four million dollars," Jason added.

Kate looked surprised. "The offer's gone up."

"Jason couldn't help overhearing," Abbie apologized.

"Big Tony's sitting with the Noonans. They could afford to buy in. Tib Noonan is one of New York City's top neurologists."

"Jody seems pretty upset by the whole thing," Todd said, gulping the last of his fresh-squeezed orange juice.

"We all are," Kate replied. "Wolf River Lodge here, the Parker House at the west end of the lake. That's it. Algonquin Lake is surrounded by wild land—nearly one hundred miles of unspoiled shoreline. Big Tony's Osprey Club would destroy the wilderness character of the whole area. And it would kill a much more meaningful project, one that might even bring the wolf back to the Adirondacks."

"Bring the wolf back?" Jason practically shouted. "That would be cool!"

Big Tony's melon-shaped head shot up from his blueprints. He stared at Jason, then began to laugh. "If the wolves come back, sonny, they'll be stuffed over my fireplaces."

Big Tony shook his head and returned his attention to his prospective investor.

"What do you mean, wolves?" Abbie asked seriously.

"The Blackstone estate is one of a dozen private parcels north of the lake," Kate continued. "All are adjacent to public land, all designated wilderness areas. If the state could purchase these key private parcels, it could create a new, half-million acre wilderness area large enough to support a population of wolves."

"You can't be serious," Todd said.

"It's working in Yellowstone; it can work here," she continued. "Just imagine the thrill of listening to the wild cry of a wolf in the Adirondacks for the first time in a hundred years."

"Will the Spirit Wolf come back, too?" Jason asked.

Kate patted him on the head.

"The Spirit Wolf is here, Jason," she said, pointing to her heart. "We just can't see him."

Oh, no, not another screwball, Todd thought.

She got up. "If Big Tony Delmonte pulls this deal off..." She shook her head and walked away.

Abbie pushed her plate away. "That's all for me."

Todd snared one of her sausage links.

"Me, too. Jason, how about giving those skis a try?" He looked at Abbie and crossed his fingers.

This would be a first. Bill Robinson had told them the blind can ski downhill. They simply ski with someone close by who provides a point of reference and visual guidance when needed. Cross-country skiing should be a lot easier, he said. Jason was slowly getting back into sports. He'd even played a couple of games of soccer. The ball was fitted with a beeper. Players chased the sound of the ball up and down the field. Some of the kids were pretty damn good.

Jason was anxious to try the skis. "Yeah, Dad. I can do it."

Noah Boone was sitting at his desk in the lodge office, bent over his computer keyboard.

"I see Wolf River Lodge is wired to the Information Super Highway," Todd said as they walked through the open door.

"This dang thing is still a mystery to me," Noah admitted. "I write with it, check the news, weather, that sort of thing. Jody and a college friend helped get our web site up a couple of years ago."

Abbie's attention was drawn to a large map thumb-tacked to the wall near the window. "What's the Seven Peaks Wilderness Area?" she asked.

"What could be the Seven Peaks Wilderness Area," Noah corrected her.

He got up and walked to the map.

"The green areas are existing state wilderness areas. The tan colored blocks are private holdings."

"Oh, Kate was just telling us about it," Todd said. "She said this guy, Big Tony Delmonte, is trying to buy up thousands of acres to develop."

"That's right. This is the Blackstone estate, here," Noah said, pointing to a tan triangle wedged between two green squares. "Drop a hundred homes in here, a clubhouse and restaurant, maybe even a golf course," he continued, jabbing his finger at the map, "and it's hit the road, Henry David Thoreau, and don't you come back no more."

As he swept his leathery hand over the map, the Mozart CD he was playing was obliterated by an ear-splitting whine outside the window. Three black and yellow snowmobiles shrieked away from the lodge.

Noah looked out the window. "That's Big Tony right now, heading for who-knows-where."

He watched the blue haze from the snowmobiles' exhaust drift across the driveway.

"Thoreau believed as long as we have wilderness, we have hope," he said softly. "Wilderness is the very flow of life, our evolution. It's everything that we are."

He turned from the window and rubbed his chin.

"Can't you fight him?" Abbie asked.

"All the environmental organizations are lined up against him," he said, "but Big Tony's got some very powerful friends. The governor was leaning our way, but since he began showing up in Iowa and New Hampshire, he's been silent on the issue. It's no secret he's running for president. And he needs people with money, like Big

Tony Delmonte. Give a politician a choice between wild land and campaign dollars and, well, the wild places lose every time."

He walked back to his desk.

"Wilderness is life as pure and uncomplicated as it gets. We can't make any more of it, you know."

He reached into his desk.

"Here's a trail map," he said, changing the subject. "I believe Kate suggested the Pond Loop Trail. The Spruce Ridge Trail is a little trickier. You can pick it up in back of the chapel if you want to give it a shot. It winds through a stand of old growth trees. Pretty spectacular. You'll probably see Charlie Two Shirts. He's at the chapel getting things ready for tonight's service."

"I've never met a real Indian before," Jason said.

"Charlie's pretty special. He's forgotten more about these mountains than I'll ever know."

"What's the story on Bushy Barnes?" Todd asked. "He said he grew up around here, but that's all he'd say."

Noah settled back in his chair. For a moment, it appeared he didn't hear the question.

"Don't let Colonel Barnes' backwoods pumpkin routine fool you."

"Colonel...Barnes?" Todd asked.

"Bushy was a special ops Green Beret in Vietnam, then worked for the Agency—the CIA—for twenty years."

"I'll be damned," Todd said, shaking his head.

"He's been stationed all over the world, doing, well, whatever he did for his country. His last post was in the Middle East. Something happened out there in the desert that changed him forever. He won't talk about it. He left the CIA immediately and headed home for good. That was ten years ago. He's been with us ever since."

Abbie zipped up her coat. "You just never know about people, do you?"

They headed for the door.

"I was checking the latest weather when you came in," Noah said before they could leave. "There's a whopper of a front headed our way. They're calling for snow and high winds later today. So keep a clear eye out there. We don't want to come looking for you on Christmas Eve."

While his parents were eager for Jason to try his skis, they worried about an emotional setback if things didn't go well.

"I can do it," Jason reassured his father as he snapped the toes of Jason's ski boots into their bindings.

Abbie looked at the map. The lodge's regulations were clearly spelled out:

SNOWMOBILES RESTRICTED TO SERVICE ROADS

The snowmobile trails were marked in black. The easy ski trails were shown in green dots, the more difficult ones in thick broken lines.

"It's so quiet," she whispered.

"The silence that bludgeons you dead," Todd replied.

"Where did you steal that line?" she asked.

"**The Spell of the Yukon**, by Robert Service. I found a book of his poems back in the cabin."

The Pond Loop Trail was wide and flat. A groomed ski track had been cut several inches into the hard-packed, waist-deep snow. Jason skied behind his father. At Bill Robinson's suggestion, Jason's father had attached a little bell to his fanny sack. His mother followed with encouragement.

At first, Jason struggled to keep his balance. *I guess this isn't going to be as easy as I thought,* he decided.

He tried to steady himself with his poles, lurching forward with one, then the other. He was walking more than he was skiing. He fell twice before they'd gone a hundred yards. But by listening to the bell, he was able to pick up his pace. The bell's jingle was a beacon of sorts, helping him find his way down the dark, cold trail.

"There's a little dip just ahead," his mother warned him. "Get ready."

Jason bent his knees and coasted nicely down the hill. *Piece of cake,* he thought to himself. *This is kind of fun.*

"How's that?" he shouted, proud of his monumental accomplishment.

Then he hit an unexpected bump. His skis crossed, and he tumbled face first into the snow.

His mother rushed to his side. "Jason, are you all right?

"Yeah, I'm okay," he replied, sitting dejectedly in the snow. "Maybe I should go back," he mumbled. "You guys can ski better without me."

"You're doing great," his father said. "I'll bet you've skied half a mile. The chapel can't be far."

Cr-r-ruck.

"It's the raven again!" Jason shouted.

He fought back to his feet.

The Raven is following me, he thought, *but why?* The raven called once more, flapped its wings, and disappeared into the woods.

Jason's mother brushed him off. The snow on his neck was already beginning to melt and run beneath his sweater and down his back.

What did Bill tell me? There will be times when I feel lost. Don't panic. Think my way through the problem. And trust my feelings.

"What about Charlie Two Shirts?" his mother whispered in his ear. "I thought you wanted to meet him."

Jason smiled. He hoped the Indian would be at the chapel. There was so much he wanted to ask him.

"I'll give it another try," he told his parents.

The little bell was jingling again. Jason pushed off down the trail.

Chapter Six

"Look at the view!" Abbie exclaimed.

She jammed her ski poles into the snow and pulled off her sweat-soaked stocking cap. They had reached the chapel at last.

"Mom, what are you looking at?" Jason asked.

"Oh, Jason, the mountains in the distance—they're just beautiful. And the sky is so blue. What a perfect winter day."

Todd dug into his fanny sack for the camera.

"Those mountains—they're probably the high peaks," he said, snapping off a few shots.

"The highest is Mount Marcy. Our grandfathers called it Tahawus, the Cloud Splitter."

The voice came from behind them. It was a buckwheat honey kind of voice: dark, deep, and creamy smooth. Jason spun around, almost falling out of his skis. Even he didn't hear the man approach them.

"Oh, you surprised us!" Abbie gasped. "We...didn't see anyone."

A tall, hatchet-faced man wearing a brown fur cap and a checkered green-and-black wool coat was standing just a few feet behind them.

Where did he come from, Todd wondered.

They were in the middle of a broad clearing in front of the chapel. They thought they were alone.

"I didn't mean to startle you," the man apologized.

"You must be...Charlie Two Shirts," Todd ventured.

He'd pictured a smaller, perhaps even comical figure, with a name like Charlie Two Shirts. But this man was no cigar-store Indian, and he stood well over six feet.

"That's what I'm called," the man said, "but Charlie will do just fine. And you would be the Quinn family. Bushy said you might be stopping by."

Jason tried to speak, but the lump in his throat left him tongue-tied. He felt a hand on his shoulder.

"Good morning, Jason."

"You...know my name?" Jason stammered.

"Bushy told me all about you. You are a brave one to have skied all this way."

86

From his voice, Jason knew Charlie had knelt down in front of him. He took off his right glove and touched Charlie's face. He'd never done that to a stranger before; somehow he knew Charlie wouldn't mind.

Charlie's skin was soft and surprisingly warm. Jason ran his fingers over Charlie's cheek. He could feel a long bone. He touched his nose. It was sharp and had a bend to it, like a hawk's beak, Jason thought. He took off his other glove and touched both of Charlie's cheeks. It was a wide face, Jason guessed, full of angles and edges. He reached up and touched Charlie's hat. It was fine and furry.

"What's that?" he asked.

"Muskrat," Charlie answered.

There was something else. There was a sweet smell about Charlie. Jason had never smelled it before. One thing was for sure; he'd never been around anyone quite like Charlie Two Shirts.

"Now that you've made the trip out here, how about a tour?" Charlie asked.

Abbie helped Jason snap out of his skis. They walked up a freshly-shoveled path to the chapel.

"Pierre LaFontaine wanted to duplicate the small stone churches he knew so well in Quebec," Charlie began. "He discovered a vein of granite not far from here. That's all he needed to get started."

The chapel's front door was painted bright red. It groaned from its black iron hinges as they walked into the tiny vestibule.

Charlie removed his coat and cap. He ran his long, callused fingers through his gray, shoulder-length hair.

Abbie took a closer look at him. His skin was the color of light chocolate, and his eyes were carbon black. He was sinewy and square shouldered. Abbie guessed him to be in his mid-fifties. It was hard to tell. She thought him a very handsome fellow in a noble but forbidding sort of way.

They stepped into the chapel. Light was streaming into the room from twelve long, narrow windows.

"Mom, what's it look like?" Jason asked.

"Well," she began, "it's just beautiful. There's a fireplace just behind us."

"It's made of sandstone," Charlie interjected. "The chapel walls are paneled in birch. The beams, joists, and rafters are peeled spruce."

They walked down the aisle. The pulpit was carved from a single slab of pine. The bark was left on.

"Oh!" Abbie exclaimed.

"What, Mom?"

She didn't answer.

"What is it, Mom?" Jason asked again.

"It's a stained-glass window," his father said. "It's half the size of the back wall."

"The window...it's a white wolf," his mother said.

"Does this window have anything to do with that legend about some Spirit Wolf that Bushy Barnes was telling us yesterday?" Todd asked.

A broad smile spread across Charlie's face. "It has everything to do with the legend, Mr. Quinn."

"That's what I was afraid of," Todd replied.

"Because you cannot see something does not mean that it is not so, wouldn't you agree?"

"I don't believe in the supernatural, if that's what you're asking," Todd replied.

"There is an energy that flows from these mountains," Charlie continued. "LaFontaine experienced it one day when he was building the chapel. He said he could feel someone's hands on his own as he cut and mortared the stones. He created this window so that everyone who came here might feel the same force that flowed through him that day."

"Oh," Abbie repeated, this time in a whisper.

Todd started for the door. "Ah, well, I'm sure you're busy there, Charlie. We'd better hit the old trail."

Jason pulled at his mother's sleeve. "Could we stay for awhile? I'm kind of tired."

"Come, sit for minute," Charlie said.

"Well, just for a minute," Abbie replied.

Todd groaned but did not object.

There were half a dozen stuffed chairs arranged in a semi—circle in front of the fireplace. While they removed their jackets, Charlie added a fresh log to the fire.

Jason wasn't tired. He made that up. He didn't want to leave. He wasn't sure why. He only knew he wanted to stay with Charlie. He knew Charlie would tell him more, if his father would let him.

It felt good sitting there in the big soft chair. For a moment, he forgot he was blind. He could see the flames dancing in the fire. Or was he dreaming again?

"Mr. Quinn, my medicine tells me you are troubled by this," Charlie said with the sweep of his hand.

"Well, I gotta tell you, Charlie, this Spirit Wolf sounds like bad medicine to me," Todd said, laughing at his own joke.

Charlie smiled. If he was offended, he didn't show it.

Abbie shook her head. She had questions, but she was almost afraid to ask them. She didn't want to set her husband off. He was already picking up steam. Too many things were beginning to connect, or was her imagination playing a cruel trick on her? The Spirit Wolf appeared to have touched everyone. The stained-glass window was proof of that. She wondered if Wolf River Lodge might be a sanctuary for some freak religious cult. Or was the Spirit Wolf nothing more than a conspiracy, a hoax dreamed up by the Boone family to promote their lodge? Or could there...was there really something out there?

"Charlie," she began, "what do you mean, your medicine?"

Before he could answer, Todd's cell phone began ringing inside his jacket.

"Hello? Hey, Paul. No problem. Just a sec." He covered the phone with his hand. "I asked Paul to call me when the pricing came through on our new tissue valves. I hope I don't lose him." He pulled himself out of the chair and walked toward the vestibule. "I've got to talk to him."

Abbie gave Charlie an apologetic look.

"My medicine, Mrs. Quinn, Jason, is the energy that connects me to all of life. It teaches me that Earth is our mother. Her spirit is the flow of life that moves through all living things."

Abbie squirmed in her chair. She wasn't sure where all this was heading.

"Kate Boone told us a Catholic priest would be here tonight," she said. "This is a real chapel, isn't it?"

"Oh, it's real, Mrs. Quinn," Charlie continued. "Oh God of our salvation; who art the hope of all the ends of the earth and the farthest seas; who by thy strength hast established the mountains, being girded with might; who dost still the roaring of the seas, the roaring of the waves, the tumult of the peoples, so that those who dwell at earth's farthest bounds are afraid of thy signs. The Psalms, Mrs. Quinn."

Abbie was stunned. She didn't know what to make of this surprisingly articulate man. Perhaps there was more to Wolf River Lodge than met the eye.

"What's the connection, then, between God and this Spirit Wolf, or whatever it is?"

"The Spirit Wolf calls to us from a world beyond our own. The path to its power, like the path to God, is faith. The Spirit Wolf, Mrs. Quinn, Jason, is the connection."

Jason was scratching his head. "I don't get it," he blurted out.

Charlie smiled. "Look at it this way. We share the miracle of life with all of nature's creatures, with every living thing. We are all brothers and sisters. The birds and the animals, even the trees, all have their own medicine, their own power if you will. Their magic, their power surrounds us whenever we are one with nature."

Jason pulled himself up in his chair. "Animals can't talk," he stated matter-of-factly.

Charlie placed his hands on Jason's shoulders. "Our brothers and sisters will share their magic with us, Jason, if we take the time to listen. They speak to us in many ways, some with their voices, others simply by their actions."

"I heard a raven this morning outside my bedroom window," Jason began. "It went **Cr-r-ruck. Cr-r-ruck.** It followed us to the lodge. I heard it again in the woods before we got here. Was it...talking to me?"

"Ah, Raven." Charlie gazed into the fire. "The old ones tell us Raven is the messenger of magic."

Abbie was relieved when Todd returned from his phone call.

Thank God, she thought. *Let's get out of here.*

"Todd, if we're going to ski that other trail, we'd better get going," she said.

"The Spruce Ridge Trail has two steep sections. It'll be too difficult for our little warrior," Charlie said. "Jason can stay here with me by the fire. Bushy will be by in an hour or so. He can bring Jason back to the lodge."

Abbie was aghast at the thought.

"I think we'd better move on," Todd said.

But Jason wanted to stay. He was just beginning to understand what Charlie was talking about. He wanted to know more about the raven, about the magic of the animals, and most of all, he wanted to know more about the Spirit Wolf.

"Oh, Mom, can I stay, please?"

"Thanks, Mr. Two Shirts—I mean Charlie—but I'm sure you have things to do," Abbie replied.

"Please, Mom, please?"

Charlie smiled at Abbie and nodded reassuringly. Her misgivings immediately vanished.

"Jason, we'll see you back at the cabin," she stammered.

"Abbie!" Todd protested.

"No, Todd, it's all right. Jason will be more comfortable here." *Why did I say that?* She felt like Charlie had put the words in her mouth.

"Jason, I'm sure you'll have a wonderful time," she added. "Come on, Todd, let's get going."

"Abbie, are you nuts, leaving Jason alone with this guy?" Todd whispered as they left the chapel.

She stared at him for a moment. Her eyes were red and moist. "I don't know, Todd," she replied. "I just have this feeling this was supposed to happen. Don't ask me why. I just know it's okay."

While Charlie walked outside to point Todd and Abbie in the right direction, Jason slid his chair closer to the fire. His headaches were getting worse, but he'd decided not to tell his parents. He didn't want to spend Christmas Eve in bed.

"How about some hot chocolate?"

Jason was startled. He didn't hear Charlie walk back into the room.

"Sounds great," he answered.

"There's still a chill in here," Charlie said. "Let's go back to my place. I think you'll be more comfortable in front of the wood stove."

"You mean...the caboose?" Jason asked.

"That's right," Charlie replied. "I've got something to show you."

Jason stood and reached out with his right hand. He found Charlie's elbow waiting for him.

"It's snowing," Jason said, "isn't it, Charlie? I can feel it on my face."

Charlie looked into the gunmetal-gray sky.

"That storm's moving in fast."

"I hope my parents will be okay," Jason said.

"Don't worry; they should be back at the lodge in forty-five minutes or so."

The old red caboose was tucked into the edge of the woods about a hundred yards from the chapel. Charlie helped Jason over the metal stairway and onto a small platform. He climbed up and opened the door.

"You can sit in my rocking chair. I'll get that hot chocolate started."

"What's that smell?" Jason asked.

It was the same smell he'd noticed when Charlie surprised them in front of the chapel. Only now it was much stronger.

"That's sage and cedar. Sage draws out negative energy," Charlie explained. "The cedar attracts positive energy."

Jason took a long, deep breath. A warm sweetness filled his lungs. He felt a little light-headed, too.

"It'll take just a minute to warm up the milk," Charlie said.

"What's your caboose look like?" Jason asked.

"My desk is to your left," Charlie began. "I added a large window—nice view of the mountains. There's a window in back of you, too. That's where the brakeman sat to watch the train. My bed's between here and the kitchen. The bathroom, well, that's a little walk out into the woods."

He placed a warm mug in Jason's hands.

"Be careful; the hot chocolate's a little too hot."

Jason took a short sip. "Tastes good, Charlie."

"Tell me about your blindness. Perhaps I can help you."

Jason was startled by Charlie's remark. *What does he mean, perhaps he can help me?* Jason explained his accident.

"Dr. Kerr told me I can't see because my brain is hurt," Jason concluded. "He said I might get better. I might not. So I should learn to live a new way."

"So how do you think you're doing?" Charlie asked.

"Okay, I guess. I miss my friends. They don't come around much anymore. My parents are having a hard time with me—I can tell."

"What frightens you the most?" Charlie asked.

"I guess when I'm in bed, when I'm alone. It's so quiet. When I can't hear anything, I feel really lost. And when I get up in the morning—when I open my eyes—it's still dark. It's like it's always the middle of the night."

He wiped his eyes with the sleeve of his sweater and took another sip of hot chocolate. He felt Charlie's warm hand on his shoulder.

"What makes you happy?" Charlie asked. "Is there a time you forget about your blindness, for just a little while?"

"This might sound sort of crazy, but when I'm outside, sometimes I think I see things. It's just my memory—that's what Dr. Kerr said. Like last night, there was a shooting star. I was sure I saw it, but I know I really didn't. And afterward, I felt kind of funny."

"You did see it, Jason, just in a different way," Charlie said. "You felt it in your heart."

"My mom has a garden outside our porch," Jason continued. "I remember these tall purple bushes. They're butterfly bushes, I think. I can't watch the butterflies anymore, but I can still smell the flowers. But when I'm sitting there in the garden, I can almost see the butterflies, too."

He drank some more hot chocolate.

"I guess when I'm outside, it just doesn't seem so dark anymore."

"That's not surprising," Charlie said.

"What do you mean?" Jason asked.

"Remember what I said earlier, Jason? There is an energy that flows through all living things. The birds, the trees, the animals in the forest, you and me—we are all connected by this energy. It is the spirit of life, Jason. When we walk in the woods or sit quietly by a stream, when we feel the wind on our hair or the sun dancing off our face, when we are truly one with nature—the connection can be very powerful. If we open our hearts, Jason, the energy will flow to us."

Jason sat perfectly still, as if in a trance.

What was Charlie saying? Was there some power, some force that might…help him see again? *No, that can't be it, can it?*

"Jason, when Raven called to you, it was asking you a question."

"A question?" Jason asked. "What question?"

Jason felt Charlie place something in his lap. It was soft: a pouch of some kind, Jason thought, about the size of a small gym bag. There were strings, like leather shoelaces, at one end. It wasn't heavy, but it was filled with, well, things.

"What is it?" he asked.

"It's my medicine bag," Charlie replied.

"You mean like a doctor's bag?" Jason asked.

"Well, you might say that. It's made of deerskin, Jason. And what's inside connects me to the Creator, to all of Earth's energy."

"How will the bag help me answer raven's question?" Jason asked.

"Open it," Charlie whispered. "Let your heart tell you what to take out."

Jason untied the bag and reached inside. He touched a feather, some small stones. There were sharp objects; others were soft, like pieces of fur. He felt something like a shell. He took it out. There were little ridges along the top. It was smooth on the other side. He turned it in his hand. His heart was beating faster. He wondered what kind of a game Charlie was playing with him.

"It feels like some sort of shell," Jason said.

"It is a turtle shell, Jason."

"What does that mean?"

"Mother Earth was born when Turtle rose from the sea," Charlie began. "The mountains and the forests grew on turtle's back. That is why my people, all the Mohawk, call our home Turtle Island. Turtle has touched your heart. That tells us that you believe in the sacredness of Mother Earth. You believe that she can heal you and protect you."

Jason was stunned. *Heal me? Protect me? No one has ever said that to me,* he thought, *not even Bill.*

"Please, Jason, another object," Charlie urged him.

Jason dug back into the medicine pouch. He felt around until something pricked him on the finger.

"Ouch!" he cried.

He pulled out whatever it was still stuck to his finger.

"Ah, a porcupine quill," Charlie said. "This is good."

"Good?" Jason asked. "It hurts."

"Quills protect Porcupine when a trust is broken between beings. Porcupine tells us that you must always trust your faith in the power of your medicine."

Jason pulled the quill out and touched his finger to his lips. There was no blood.

"Porcupine is the cabin we are staying in," he said.

"Interesting," Charlie said. "Now, a third object, please."

Jason reached back into the bag. He touched the feather again. It was a small feather, about the length of his hand. He took it out. His eyes began to burn. It wasn't an intense pain, more like specks of dust were floating around in there somewhere.

"You have found Owl's feather," Charlie told him. "Owl hunts at night. Owl sees what others cannot see. What do you think this means, Jason?"

Jason was almost afraid to ask. He wiped at his eyes. "Does it mean I will have the eyes of Owl?" Jason asked.

"It means that you are not afraid of the dark. You already see things, feel things others cannot," Charlie continued. "Reach into the bag one more time."

Jason felt a round stone, then a carved piece of wood. He rolled it in his hand but let it go. *There's something, an arrowhead, I think. No it doesn't feel right.* He let it go, too. *What's this?*

It was sharp, like a claw. He took it out. His heart was pounding. Sweat was running into his eyes. He blinked and rubbed at his face with his sleeve.

"What is it?" he asked Charlie. "It feels like a claw."

"You have found the talon of Eagle," Charlie replied.

"Eagle teaches us to look higher, beyond what others can see. Eagle tests your faith like no other."

Jason ran his fingers over each of the talons. *How high, how far did eagle fly?* He took Turtle's shell, Porcupine's quill, and Owl's feather from his lap and held them with Eagle's talon.

"My medicine tells me your faith is strong, Jason. You have answered Raven's question."

"What was Raven's question?" Jason asked.

"By your actions, by your words, you have told Raven that yes, you do believe in the magic of life."

Jason felt Charlie replace the objects in his hands with something round. It felt like it was made of sticks and was about the size of the palm of his hand. It was light as a feather. There was a web in the middle of the circle, made of strips of leather, Jason thought. There was a carved stone in the middle of the web. He explored it with his fingers. He picked it up and smelled it.

"It is a Christmas gift for you," Charlie said.

Jason ran his fingers over it again. "What is it?"

"It's a dream catcher, Jason. The circle is made of willow twigs. The web is tied with strips of tanned deer hide."

"What's the stone in the middle?" Jason asked. "It feels like, some kind of animal. Is it…is it a wolf?"

Jason felt Charlie's hand on his forehead.

"It's the Spirit Wolf, Jason," Charlie began. "Your blindness has opened your heart to a world you never knew. Hang the dream catcher where you sleep, my little brother, and your dreams will come true."

Jason ran his fingers over the stone. "Charlie, if I hang the dream catcher over my bed, will the Spirit Wolf come?"

Charlie gave him a hug. "The Spirit Wolf is here, now."

"Where?" Jason cried out.

"Listen to your heart, Jason, and you will hear its call."

Jason wanted to know more, but suddenly cocked his head. "I hear a snowmobile."

"It's Bushy, back with those propane tanks," Charlie replied. "Let's go down and meet him."

When they reached the chapel, Bushy had the tanks unloaded and hooked up.

"Hi, partner," Bushy began. "Saw your parents on their way back to the lodge. They said you'd hung back here with Charlie."

Jason reached into his pocket. "Look what Charlie gave me."

"Ah, dream catcher," Bushy replied. "Better be careful where you hang that. Never know what might happen," he added with a hearty laugh. "We'd better get you back to your parents. They'll begin to think you and Charlie here lit out for parts unknown."

"You might say we did," Charlie said with wink.

Bushy fired the engine.

"Hold on tight!" he shouted.

Jason dug his fingers into Bushy's thick wool coat. He had never ridden a snowmobile before. The wind slashed at his face like an icy whip. Water surged from his eyes, but he didn't dare let go of Bushy to wipe them.

"Hey, this is neat!" he yelled. He thought he heard Bushy laughing, but he wasn't sure over the roar of the engine.

Then the snowmobile slowed.

Are we there already? Jason wondered.

"Got to stop at the gas shed," Bushy called back. "We're running on fumes. Looks like Big Tony and his family are filling up, too"

Bushy brought the snowmobile to a stop. "Where you heading, Big Tony?"

"Making a run to the Parker House," Big Tony bellowed. "Grab a beer or three. Where have you been, boy?" he shouted at Jason.

"I've been with Charlie Two Shirts," Jason replied proudly. "He gave me a magic dream catcher for Christmas!"

"That old redskin!" Big Tony howled.

But even Jason couldn't hear what else Big Tony shouted at him as he fired his engine.

"Snow's coming down pretty good," Bushy yelled back at him. "Better not stay up there too long."

Big Tony gunned his engine and shot away from the pump. "See you in church!" he yelled back.

"What did Big Tony mean about Charlie?" Jason asked.

"Ah, nothing," Bushy replied. "Just beer talk."

"What's the Parker House?"

"Bar and restaurant about fifteen miles from here at the other end of the lake. Big Tony's sticking his neck out riding all the way up there with his family in this kind of weather, and it's only going to get worse."

Bushy decided to leave the snowmobile at the gas shed and walk Jason back to the cabin.

"Is that man, Big Tony, going to kill all the animals?" Jason asked as they tramped up the river trail. It had already snowed a couple of inches.

"Kill the animals?" Bushy asked. "Oh, you mean his development, that Osprey Club he wants to build?"

"Yeah," Jason replied. "He said all the wolves would be stuffed."

"Well, Jason, Big Tony's got a lot of powerful people in his back pocket, so to speak. Selfish, greedy people who couldn't care less what this country looks like fifty or a hundred years from now."

Abbie opened the door as they walked onto the deck.

"Here he is," Bushy announced. "Safe and sound."

Abbie helped Jason off with his coat.

"You can ride the bobsled to the chapel tonight if you like," Bushy informed her. "Jeb and Joe and I will start our little shuttle service from the lodge about five-thirty or so."

"Oh, we'll see you then," she replied.

Abbie felt Jason's forehead. *He's burning up,* she thought.

"Did you and Dad have fun?" Jason asked.

"We had a wonderful ski," she replied. "And what did you and Charlie Two Shirts do after we left?"

Todd looked up from the couch. He was sprawled there in front of the fire with his first Canadian Club of the day.

Jason reached into his shirt pocket. "Look what Charlie gave me."

"What in hell is that?" Todd asked.

Abbie leaned over for a closer look.

"It's a dream catcher. Charlie told me if I hang it over my bed, the Spirit Wolf will come."

"Oh, no, that's what I was afraid of," Todd said, getting up off the couch. "What else did he tell you?"

"We went to his caboose."

"You went where?"

"We went to his caboose, and I took things from his medicine bag. We talked about animals, about...their magic powers."

"That's it, Jason. I don't want you to see him again!" Todd shouted.

"Todd," Abbie pleaded. "He's not feeling well."

"Jason, this Charlie Two Shirts—or whatever his real name is—he's not a doctor. A witch doctor maybe, but not a real doctor," Todd said, lowering his voice. "He has no right to fill your head with...who knows what."

Abbie wrapped her arm around Jason. "You've had a big day, and we still have church and dinner. Why don't you rest for a while here on the couch?"

She covered him with a thick red-and-black Hudson's Bay Company blanket. Jason was asleep almost instantly.

"I'm worried about him," Abbie admitted.

"This sacred wilderness jive has gone too far," Todd replied. "These people are all nuts."

Abbie picked up his glass and took a sip of his drink.

"I know what you're thinking, Todd," she began, "but this Charlie Two Shirts is, well, he's a very articulate and, I think, religious person. I don't think he'd do anything to harm Jason."

"Oh, Jesus, don't tell me you're falling for this Spirit Wolf crap," Todd replied. "The last thing Jason needs is some self-appointed holy man getting into his head."

"I don't know what to believe anymore," she admitted. "There just seem to be too many coincidences. Too many things are beginning to connect."

She took the dream catcher from Jason's hand.

"Like this dream catcher," she continued. "It looks just like the wolf in the stained-glass window."

"What next?" Todd mumbled as he headed for the kitchen to refill his drink.

Chapter Seven

Jason felt his mother's long soft fingers stroking his forehead.

"You've been asleep for two hours."

"Mom, what time is it?"

"About five-thirty. How are you feeling?"

Jason yawned. "I'm okay, I guess."

"What do you mean, I guess?" his father asked.

"I don't know," Jason replied. "I've sort of felt funny all day. I have a little headache."

"We could skip church and bring our dinner back here," his mother offered.

"Good idea," his father said.

"No, I want to go," Jason insisted. "I'll be all right."

It was snowing hard when they left for the lodge.

Noah Boone was right about that storm, Todd thought. He kicked at the fresh snow.

"I'll bet we got three inches in the last couple of hours," he said.

"I hear sleigh bells!" Jason cried out.

"Bushy's pulling up in front of the lodge now, and he's dressed like Santa himself," Todd replied. "Come on; we don't want to miss our ride."

Bushy had trimmed the bobsled with strings of green and blue lights. Even Jeb and Joe were dressed for the occasion with red-and-white stocking caps pinned between their ears.

"All aboard!" Bushy cried out. "We don't want to be late for church."

"Are you really dressed up like Santa?" Jason asked.

"All but my beard," Bushy replied. "By golly, that's all mine. Ho, ho, ho!" he roared. "Giddap, Jeb. Giddap, Joe."

He snapped the reins. The ride to the church took just ten minutes.

"I've seen everything now," Abbie gasped.

"Mom, what?"

"The chapel's just ahead," she replied. "There must be twenty snowmobiles parked in front. Where did they all come from?"

"The Parker House, Gull Point, up that way," Bushy replied. "Father Mike always brings a bunch with him from Old Forge. That's the padre himself, coming up behind us."

A black snowmobile roared past them and slid to a stop in front of the chapel.

"Mighty fancy rig you got there, Bushy," the priest began. "You've outdone yourself this year."

"Why, thank you, Father," Bushy replied.

Father Michael Mulcahy shut off his snowmobile, climbed off, and removed his helmet. Todd guessed him to be maybe forty. He was a monstrous man with the girth of a great bear. His hair was gray, like smoke from a smoldering campfire. A thick, yellowish moustache draped his mouth.

He wore a black snowmobile suit with purple trim. A white cross and **Father Mike** were stitched over the breast pocket.

"Merry Christmas, Jason," the priest boomed. He plucked Jason down from the bobsled as if he were made of straw.

How did he know my name, Jason wondered.

Abbie looked at Todd. He shook his head.

"Follow me," Father Mulcahy said, extending his right elbow.

Jason found it immediately. They walked into the chapel.

"How did you know my name?" Jason asked.

"Oh, an angel told me," Father Mulcahy replied.

"An angel?" Jason asked.

But before the priest could answer, Jason's parents had caught up to them.

"We'd better find a seat," his mother said. "This place is filling up fast."

"Let's sit in back by the fireplace," Todd suggested.

Abbie wasn't surprised. When he did attend church with her and Jason, Todd always sat near the door, where he could be the first one out. She'd thought after Jason's accident that he might reach out for the support their church could offer. But instead he grew more cynical, more isolated from her own beliefs.

Charlie Two Shirts was tending a crackling fire.

"Merry Christmas, my little brother."

Jason reached out and touched Charlie's sleeve.

"From what I hear, you two had quite an afternoon," Todd cracked.

"That's some fire you've got going," Abbie quickly chimed in. She didn't want Todd instigating a confrontation.

"Its smoke will carry your prayers to the Creator," Charlie said with a smile.

Todd rolled his eyes. They hurried to their seats.

The prelude began. Abbie looked for the first time at the program she'd been handed at the front door. The chapel's stained-glass window—the white wolf—was featured on its cover. She took Jason's hand. Father Mulcahy rose to the bark-sheathed pulpit. He cleared his throat.

"In the days of Herod, King of Judea," he began, "there was a man named Zechariah. He had a wife named Elizabeth, and they were both righteous before God. But they had no children, because

110

Elizabeth was barren. Now while he was serving as a priest before God, it fell to him to enter the temple of the Lord and burn incense. And there appeared an angel of the Lord."

·*He's talking about angels,* Jason thought.

He tugged at his mother's sleeve and whispered, "Father Mulcahy said an angel told him I was coming tonight."

"Jason, not now," she replied softly.

"The angel said to him," the priest continued, "'Do not be afraid, Zechariah, for your prayer is heard, and your wife will bear you a son, and you shall call his name John.' And Zechariah said to the angel, 'How shall I know this?' And the angel answered him, 'I am Gabriel, who stands in the presence of God.'"

Father Mulcahy paused. "All rise."

The organist began her prelude to **O Come All Ye faithful**.

Abbie quickly thumbed through the hymnal and began to sing. Jason did his best to follow along. His father mumbled a word now and then.

"After these days, Zechariah's wife did indeed conceive," Father Mulcahy resumed his recitation. "In the sixth month, the angel was sent from God to a city of Galilee named Nazareth, to a virgin betrothed to a man whose name was Joseph, of the house of David; and the virgin's name was Mary. And he came to her and said, 'Hail, favored one; the Lord is with you.' But she was greatly troubled by the saying and considered in her mind what sort of greeting this might be. And the angel said to her, 'Do not be afraid, Mary, for you have

111

found favor with God. And behold, you will conceive in your womb and bear a son, and you shall call his name Jesus.'"

The organist, a plump, redheaded woman, signaled the start of **Hark! The Herald Angels Sing**. Her silver snowmobile boots and decal-decorated helmet were tucked beneath her seat.

She must be part of the show, Todd thought.

Jason stood for the invocation. He ran his fingers over the dream catcher he'd brought along in his pant's pocket. *Could the chimney smoke really carry my prayers to heaven, like Charlie said?* Jason wondered. He pressed the dream catcher to his lips, then put it back in his pocket.

"Are angels real?" he whispered to his mother.

"Jason, please," she replied.

"Rekindle our joy in living, refuel our passion for truth," the congregation concluded.

There was a moment of silence.

"The people who walked in darkness have seen a great light," Father Mulcahy began.

Is he talking about me? Jason wondered.

"Those who dwelt in a land of deep darkness, on them a light has shined."

What light? Does he mean the shooting star, last night? Jason wondered.

Abbie was wondering the same thing. She took her son's hand.

"For us a child is born, to us a son is given," the priest continued. "In that region there were shepherds out in the fields, keeping watch over their flocks by night. And an angel said, 'Be not afraid; for behold, I bring you news of great joy, which will come to all the people; for to you is born this day in the city of David a Savior who is Christ the Lord.'"

The choir of five women and two men stood and sang **While Shepherds Lately Watched.**

Father Mulcahy reached out to the congregation.

"Merry Christmas to all. Welcome to this most sacred of places," he began. "I see many familiar faces and, I am happy to say, some new worshipers as well. The Boone family once again invites all of us to join them at Wolf River Lodge following tonight's service. A traditional Christmas Eve dinner has been served at the lodge for what, Noah, must be a hundred years now?"

"This is year 110," Noah Boone replied from somewhere near the center of the congregation.

"Well, it only gets better," the priest replied. "I cannot think of a more appropriate place to celebrate the birth of Jesus Christ than here, in this chapel. Pierre LaFontaine believed these mountains to be sacred, for it is here that, in his own words, 'an angel lives to celebrate the glory of all life.' The Spirit Wolf, so beautifully depicted behind me, lives in the hearts of everyone who truly believes that angels are the messengers of God."

Abbie turned to Todd. "What's going on here?"

Todd raised his eyes and shook his head.

"Is the Spirit Wolf an angel?" Jason asked.

His mother put her arm around him. *What have we gotten ourselves into,* she wondered.

"We are gathered here in these beautiful mountains," Father Mulcahy continued, "because the Bible is wrong." He paused to allow his seemingly blasphemous declaration to hang over the congregation like a storm cloud.

"The Bible defines wilderness as a place without God. But we know that the power and the glory of nature must truly be the work of God. The Scriptures tell us the God who made our world and everything in it does not live in shrines made by human hands. Nature, my friends, is where God welcomes us to sit at his table. Job affirmed God's voice in nature when he said, 'But ask the beasts, and they will teach you. The birds of the air, and they will tell you. In His hand is the life of every living thing.' We nurture our bodies and cleanse our souls in the glory of His gifts, the lakes and rivers, the mountains and all their glory that surrounds us tonight."

He stepped down from his pulpit and walked into the congregation.

"No, God does not live in shrines and temples, my friends. He lives here! In these mountains!" Father Mulcahy spread his massive arms out to the congregation. "In nature, every day is Sunday!"

Everyone rose.

"You alone are the Lord. You made the heavens and all their starry host, the earth and all that is on it, the seas and all that is in them. You give life to everything and the multitudes of heaven worship you. Amen."

Father Mulcahy returned to his pulpit.

"If God speaks to us through every living thing, then does it not follow that his messengers are all around us? The word angel comes from the Greek word angelos, which means messenger. It has long been believed that angels are here to bridge the gap between God and mankind. Angels can take many forms, disguising themselves as animals, people, sometimes dreams, or simply a mysterious voice."

He turned and pointed to the stained-glass window.

"Pierre La Fontaine was not the first to believe that the Spirit Wolf is an angel, that the Spirit Wolf is a messenger of God."

Abbie thought she saw the priest's eyes flash in the soft light of chapel. She blinked. *Am I seeing things,* she wondered.

Jason pulled at her sleeve once more. "I told you, Mom."

Father Mulcahy looked over the congregation.

"Are angels real?" he asked.

"Why do some people see angels and others do not? These are questions that have been asked for centuries. To believe in angels is simply to believe. Angels connect us to all of life's mysteries. Angels do exist, through the eyes of faith. If we pray for their strength, we will find it...because angels are proof that God is real."

The congregation rose.

"We believe in Him who the rulers of the earth ignored."

Jason tugged again at his mother's arm. "Did you hear it?" he whispered.

"Hear what?" she asked.

"The wolf. I heard a wolf howl, out there," he said, pointing toward the wall.

Todd looked at his wife and shook his head. "You sure know how to pick 'em, Abbie," he whispered.

Jason stood still while the affirmation continued. He listened, not to the words, but for the call—an eerie, haunting call he was sure he heard…out there.

Then the organist began **It Came Upon a Midnight Clear**. Jason heard the door to the vestibule open, then quickly close. He felt a rush of cold air.

"Did someone come in?" he asked.

His father looked over his shoulder. "There's some guy standing there with his hat in his hand."

"Shhh," Abbie whispered, crossing her lips with a finger.

Todd watched the man walk to the fireplace. *He looks like a hippie from the sixties,* Todd thought, *one of those deadbeats that flock to Grateful Dead concerts and Spotted Owl demonstrations.*

The man had shoulder-length, shaggy brown hair. His thick beard dripped with melting snow and ice. He was about six feet tall, Todd guessed, and from his lean appearance he was a man eating sparingly.

A Deadhead, Todd thought. *Now the day is complete.*

"Stop staring," Abbie scolded him.

Todd turned and stumbled through the carol's third verse.

As candles were passed throughout the congregation, Abbie looked up again at the stained-glass window. The wolf's yellow eyes shimmered in the dancing candlelight. She looked back over her shoulder. The bearded stranger smiled back at her. She turned quickly and searched through her hymnal for **Silent Night**. The prelude began, but her eyes wandered back to the stained-glass window. She stared into the wolf's fiery eyes.

Could there really be something out there, she wondered. *Or was this some sort of dream...or nightmare?* She was surprised when she heard the benediction begin. *Did we sing the carol? What happened to **The Lord's Prayer**? Where have I been the last ten minutes?*

The service was over. Turning to leave, Todd noticed Charlie Two Shirts, Bushy Barnes, and the disheveled stranger talking in the vestibule. All three walked out together.

"I don't know about you, but I'm starved," he said. "It's been a long day."

"That man who came in toward the end of the service..." Abbie began.

"You mean the hippie?" Todd asked.

"Well, he was a scraggly fellow. I wonder where he came from."

"From what I've seen around here so far," Todd replied, "it wouldn't be a shock if he flew in from outer space."

117

They put their coats on in the vestibule, then joined the reception line that snaked its way out of the chapel. Father Mulcahy was standing on the front steps. He was hatless in the driving snow.

"Merry Christmas," he said, shaking Abbie's hand. "How did you like our little service?"

She wasn't sure how to answer.

"Oh, the chapel is just beautiful," she ventured.

"Father," Jason stammered. "I think...I think I heard the Spirit Wolf."

"Jason, all you heard was the wind," his father quickly said.

The priest looked into Jason's empty eyes. "Do you believe in angels, Jason?"

"I...I think so," he replied.

"Then perhaps what you heard was not the wind," Father Mulcahy said. "Far from it." He looked at Todd and winked.

"Over here!" Bushy cried.

They climbed into the sled.

"Who was that bearded guy you were talking to back at the chapel?" Abbie asked.

"The Deadhead," Todd added.

"Name's Lucas," Bushy began. "Says he's camping out on Loon Island."

"Camping? In the middle of winter?" Abbie asked.

"Winter camping can be downright enjoyable if you know what you're doing," Bushy replied. "No black flies, no mosquitoes—that's for sure."

"Where's Loon Island?" Todd asked.

"Up the lake, oh, six miles or so from the lodge. Beats me how he found us here on a night like this."

"Loon Island sounds like a good place for him," Todd laughed.

"Todd, please," Abbie scolded.

"Interesting fella," Bushy continued. "See for yourself." He pointed over his shoulder.

The stranger was running toward the sled. He wore a tattered, black wool coat. Its white lining hung in shreds from half a dozen rips in the arms and chest. His red longjohns were clearly visible through a gaping hole in his baggy gray wool pants. But his shaggy appearance was deceiving. There was a purposeful, catlike rhythm to his stride. He handed Bushy a pair of snowshoes and leapt into the sled.

"Hello, Jason," he said softly.

"How did you know my name?" Jason asked. *How does everyone around here know my name,* he kept asking himself.

"Charlie Two Shirts was telling me about you."

There was an awkward silence.

Jason thought he smelled pine needles on the man's clothing.

Todd sighed and at last introduced Abbie and himself. They did not shake hands. The man called Lucas simply nodded and smiled.

"I didn't catch your last name," Todd said.

"Oh," the stranger replied, "Lucas will do just fine."

Bushy snapped the reins. "Snow's coming down to beat the band," he shouted from the front seat. "Bet we got half a foot since this afternoon."

Several snowmobiles snarled past them. The horses slogged on, oblivious to the oily intrusion.

"Where you from there, Lucas?" Todd wouldn't give up.

"Oh, just passing through," he replied.

Not much of an answer, Todd thought. *I'll try again.*

"What do you do? For a living, I mean."

"Oh, I find what I can here and there."

A bum, just as I thought, Todd decided.

Abbie didn't like Jason sitting next to this man. *Who knows where he's been,* she worried. *Thank God it's just a short ride to the lodge.*

"Jason," Lucas began, "Charlie Two Shirts said you skied all the way out to the chapel this afternoon."

"Yeah, Jason answered, "but I fell a few times."

"Don't be discouraged," Lucas continued. "Let nature work its magic on you."

Oh, no, Todd thought. *Jason doesn't need another head case working him over.* He wanted to change the subject.

"So how long will you be camping on the island?"

"I'll be moving on sometime tomorrow."

"I heard a wolf tonight!" Jason suddenly blurted out. "Did you hear it, Mr. Lucas?"

"Come on, Jason," his father interrupted. "All you heard was the wind. I told you that already."

"Aaah, oooooo!" Lucas suddenly cried. "Aaah, aaah, oooooo!"

"Just like that!" Jason shouted. "Was that you, just fooling around, Mr. Lucas?"

Lucas smiled and winked at Todd and Abbie.

A chill ran down Abbie's spine.

"Aaah, oooooo!" Jason cried.

He was still practicing his wolf calls when Bushy brought the sled to a stop in front of the lodge.

"Want to give me a hand with the horses, Lucas?" Bushy asked.

Lucas said nothing but jumped effortlessly into the front seat. The two rode off.

Todd swung the lodge door open. Noah Boone was seated at the small, roll-top desk that served as the lodge's nerve center. He was on the telephone. Big Tony Delmonte's wife, Tina, and her son, Joey, were standing over him. Jason could smell the oil on their snowmobile suits.

"The bar is open," Todd declared. "I'll catch up to you in the dining room."

He hoped he wouldn't run into Big Tony again. Four men were playing cards at a small table in the corner of the bar. Their snowmobile suits and helmets were hanging nearby. Two men and a woman were at the bar. Todd recognized them from the chapel. There was no sign of Big Tony Delmonte. Todd ordered his usual— only this time he made it a double. He took an eye-watering swallow, then headed for the dining room.

Kate Boone greeted him at the door.

"What's going on?" he asked, nodding at the crowd now gathered in the lobby.

"Big Tony Delmonte is missing," she replied. "Noah's on the phone with the ranger station at Gull Point."

Noah hung up the phone. He patted Tina Delmonte on the shoulder, then motioned for his wife to join them.

Todd caught up with Abbie and Jason at their usual table.

"That guy, Big Tony Delmonte, is apparently missing," Todd said as he sat down.

"Mr. Delmonte was getting gas for his snowmobile when Bushy and I came back from the chapel," Jason said. "He told us he'd see us in church."

Abbie shook her head. "What a terrible way to spend Christmas Eve: lost in a snowstorm in the middle of nowhere."

"Here comes Jody," Todd said. "Maybe she knows something."

"We have smoked ham and roast beef on the buffet, and leave room for our custard pudding," she announced as she filled their water glasses. "It's a lodge specialty."

"Your mom told us Big Tony Delmonte is missing," Todd began. "Have you heard anything?"

"His wife said they left the Parker House about four o'clock."

"How far is that?" Abbie asked.

"About fifteen miles. Mrs. Delmonte said her husband was riding in front, maybe seventy-five yards or so. She could barely see him the way the snow was blowing. All of sudden, he sped ahead and disappeared. She and Joey got disoriented in the snow, rode around in circles a couple of times, and finally got back here half an hour ago. No sign of Big Tony, though."

"How awful," Abbie said. "What are they going to do?"

"We usually call in a helicopter from Fort Drum, but in this weather, even the US Army is grounded."

"I'll bet Charlie could find him," Jason suggested.

"Well, if anyone can, it's Charlie Two Shirts," Jody replied. "Dad called Mary Ann—she owns the Parker House—and she said it's a total whiteout up there. Charlie said he'd try anyway. He left a few minutes ago."

She turned to take care of another table. "I'll let you know if I hear anything."

"Jason, would you like ham or roast beef?" his mother asked. "I'll fix you a plate."

"Ham sounds good, Mom."

He groped around the table until he found his ice water. His head was pounding.

What did he hear back there, he wondered. *Was it the Spirit Wolf, or was it that man, Lucas, trying to trick me? Or was it just the wind, like Dad said?*

He was sure he heard a wolf.

Isn't that what Charlie said about the magic of life? Didn't Father Mulcahy say that angels are real, so the Spirit Wolf must be real?

He rubbed his head. Even his eyes hurt.

"Jason, here's your dinner. Jason?" his mother asked.

"Are you okay?" his father said.

"I was just thinking about some stuff," he replied.

"I hope it wasn't about wolves," his father began. "Maybe there are angels; maybe not. I don't know. But there's no white wolf running around out there, that's for sure."

"But I heard it, Dad. I really did!"

"Jason," his father began, almost shouting, "I want you to stop this nonsense right now!"

"Your dinner is right in front of you, Jason," his mother said. "I cut up the ham for you. There are some mashed potatoes, and I got you some corn. There's also a fruit cup. It's on your right. Everything looks delicious."

Jason reached for his fork.

"I'm going to grab a beer," Todd said. "How about a glass of wine?" he asked Abbie.

"I'd love a Merlot, or something like it." She waited for him to leave the table.

"Jason, this has been quite a day for you—for all of us."

She reached over and caressed the back of his head.

"That Indian, Charlie Two Shirts—you can't believe the things he's told you about animals and their powers. They simply aren't true. And this man, Lucas—I wish he'd just go away. There is no magic, Jason. Your eyesight could come back over time. We just don't know. If it does, it won't because of some Spirit Wolf, some angel, or whatever it's supposed to be."

She continued rubbing his head. She hoped what she'd just said was sinking in. She hoped Jason believed her because she wasn't sure she believed herself.

"Mom," Jason cried softly, "I heard a wolf. I know I heard a wolf."

She was wiping the tears from his eyes when Todd returned with their drinks.

"The bartender said this storm—"

Abbie put a finger to her lips before he could finish.

Todd nodded, sank into his chair, and looked around the room. It was almost full. The Blackstone woman and her friends had taken a large table near the window. Tib Noonan and his wife were seated nearby. Father Mulcahy was comforting Tina and Joey Delmonte. They were seated at a table just inside the doorway. Bushy and Lucas walked in and sat down near the kitchen door.

Abbie kept dinner moving as quickly as she could.

"I've got an idea," Todd said, soaking up the last of his gravy with a roll.

"Why don't I head back for the cabin and stoke up the fire? You guys can finish up and bring dessert back. We can have it in front of our own fireplace."

Abbie looked at Todd and nodded.

"I'd like that a lot, Mom," Jason said.

"Any news?" Abbie asked when Jody returned with their desserts in Styrofoam boxes.

"Charlie just got back," she replied. "He made it to Loon Island. That's all. He said it was blowing so hard he might have ridden right past Big Tony and never seen him. There's just nothing anyone can do until morning."

Jason clung to his mother's elbow as they made their way down the lodge's snow-covered steps. The ever-present deer scampered off into the shadows.

"Thank God for the floodlights," she told Jason. "We'd never find the trail without them."

They reached the edge of the river when Jason stopped suddenly. He pulled at his mother's coat.

"What is it?" she asked.

"I heard it again."

"You heard what? The wolf?"

"Mom, I know I heard it this time."

Then he heard the wild cry again!

The wolf was out there, somewhere in the swirling snow. Now he was sure of it.

"Didn't you hear it, Mom?

She tried to listen. She heard something, but it was just the wind, she thought.

"We'd better get back to the cabin while we can still find it," she joked.

Todd was waiting for them at the door. "Get in here before you get blown away."

He put their desserts on the table in front of the fireplace.

"I'll get some plates and silverware while you guys warm up."

"Mom, I think I'll get ready for bed first," Jason sighed.

His mother followed him until he reached the bathroom.

"I'll put your pajamas out and turn down the bed. Dessert will be ready when you are."

Todd was warming a snifter of Cognac by the fire.

"How's he doing?"

Abbie collapsed into the couch. "He said he heard that wolf again on our way back from the lodge."

She put her head on his shoulder. "My God, Todd, what's going on here? I almost thought I heard it, too."

"The Spirit Wolf?" he asked.

"I don't know what it was. I think it's what you said; it's just the wind."

He swirled his Cognac in the firelight, skipped the sniff, and took a long sip.

"Like I said, Abbie, you sure can pick 'em. I don't like what's going on here, but we're stuck until tomorrow, at least."

Abbie got up from the couch. "It's too quiet back there. I'd better check."

Jason had crawled into bed and was already asleep. She pulled the covers up around him. The dream catcher was sticking out of his pajama pocket. She took it out and turned it over in her hand.

There was a framed pen-and-ink drawing of a loon hanging on the wall behind Jason's bed. She took it down and hung the dream catcher in its place.

What the heck, she thought.

She kissed him and turned out the light.

Chapter Eight

Jason tugged at his sheets, inching his way deeper under the covers. The windows shook and clattered as the storm pounded like a heavyweight's fists against the bedroom wall. He rolled on his side, curling into a ball of boy and blankets.

Would the wolf call again? He listened. And he fell to sleep.

He could see the wolf as clearly as if he were standing at the edge of the lake. It was a remarkably large male: three feet at the shoulders and weighing more than 120 pounds. But for the fire in its amber-yellow eyes, this wolf was pure white. Its footprint was enormous: nearly six inches square. A web of skin between each of its toes allowed the wolf to almost float over the snow.

This wolf had been traveling since sunrise, covering as much as twenty miles without breaking stride, occasionally hitting bursts of forty miles per hour. There was a purpose to its journey. Its destination had been clear from the start. It sniffed the air. This was the place. Loon Island. The wolf turned its back on the wind that shrieked down the lake. Jason watched as it burrowed deep into a snowbank beneath a spruce thicket on the leeward edge of the island. The wolf tucked its nose between it legs. Its thick tail sheltered its face. The wolf rested. But its ears never slept, and they had suddenly pricked forward.

The wolf's wait was over.

The snowmobile was more than two miles away, but to the wolf it was thundering toward the island like a locomotive. Jason watched as the wolf stood on its long, almost spindly legs. It shook the snow from it back, raised its head, and cried across the great emptiness. The mountains embraced its seductive call, for it had not been heard in nearly a century.

The wolf loped out onto the ice and into the path of the snowmobile. It wanted to be seen by the rider.

And soon the chase was on. The wolf headed for the north shore of the lake about a half mile away. It knew it could not outrun the snowmobile. That was not its intention. The wolf looked over its shoulder. The snowmobile and its rider had closed the distance to less than fifty yards. The wolf dashed onto the rock-strewn beach and disappeared into a stand of wind-whipped spruce trees. The snowmobile was momentarily airborne as its rider accelerated off the beach and plowed through a narrow opening in the trees.

The chase continued for two miles over the old Cedar River Snowmobile Trail. Closed for nearly five years, the trail was mostly overgrown with knee-high hemlocks and red spruce saplings. Jason was surprised that the snowmobile was gaining on the wolf over the twisting trail. Or was the wolf purposely slowing?

The trail straightened. The rider crushed the throttle in his right fist. When he saw the sign – **STOP! BRIDGE OUT. BARRIER AHEAD.**—it was already too late. Four, eight-inch thick steel pipes were stretched across the trail. Each pipe was threaded through three 8x10-inch oak posts secured in four feet of crushed stone and concrete.

The quarter-ton snowmobile disintegrated into a fiery shower of fiberglass and twisted aluminum. Miraculously, the rider was thrown clear of the barrier.

The wolf exploded out of the deep snow on the opposite bank. It stopped just long enough to watch Big Tony Delmonte crawl from the ice-jammed river; then it vanished like a ghost.

Jason rolled over and tucked his arm under his pillow. He thought he heard the door open.

"Is that you, Mom?"

Then he smelled the pine needles.

"Merry Christmas, Jason."

"Mister—I mean, Lucas—is that you?"

Jason reached out and found a wet wool sleeve. It smelled and felt just like the stranger's coat in the sled after church.

"What are you doing here?" Jason asked.

"Do you mind if I sit awhile?" Lucas asked.

Jason felt the stranger's soft, warm hand on his forehead.

"I just had a dream," Jason began, rubbing the sleep from his eyes. "Mr. Delmonte was chasing the Spirit Wolf on his snowmobile. It crashed."

"Oh, he'll be okay for a while," Lucas said.

Jason laughed. "It was just a dream."

"Are you sure, Jason?" Lucas began. "Your blindness has opened your heart to a world you have never known. You are now able to look beyond what others can see."

"That's what Charlie told me," Jason said.

"Jason, that wasn't the wind you heard tonight."

"Was it...the Spirit Wolf, Lucas? It wasn't you, fooling around?"

"I wasn't fooling around, Jason."

"Then the Spirit Wolf is real?"

"Jason, life is the magic that flows through all living things. It is the mystery that connects us to all of creation. You feel its magic every time nature speaks to you. You felt it yesterday, when Raven called to you, and today, when Charlie shared his medicine with you. And yes, you heard it tonight when the Spirit Wolf called to you. God has given every living thing the power to share its spirit, its energy, its magic, if we only take the time to listen."

"Can the Spirit Wolf help me...see again?"

"Jason, you are surrounded by the most powerful healing force imaginable. You have already been touched by its energy."

"Touched by its energy?"

"Nature can be your healer," Lucas continued, "because you are nature."

"I don't understand."

"When we are one with nature, when we embrace the beauty that surrounds us, we feel, well, free. Why do you think this is so?"

"Because of...the magic?" Jason ventured.

"That's right. When we are one with nature, we are home. In our mind we know this, and where our mind goes, our body will surely follow."

Jason felt Lucas begin to gently massage his forehead.

"You have the strength to heal yourself, Jason, but you must trust your feelings. Lift your eyes to the mountains. From where does your help come? It comes from the Lord, maker of heaven and earth."

Jason could feel Lucas get up off the edge of the bed.

"I'll see you tomorrow."

"Please don't go," Jason pleaded.

Jason heard the door close. Then a haunting call rose sharply outside his window. Its wild music rolled through the trees and echoed across the frozen lake.

He bolted up from the bedcovers.

"The Spirit Wolf!" he screamed. "It's the Spirit Wolf!"

The bedroom door opened.

"Jason, what's the matter?" his mother asked.

"I just heard it again, Mom. The Spirit Wolf!"

"Jason, you're sopping wet." She wiped his head with a corner of the bed sheet.

"Mr. Delmonte was chasing the Spirit Wolf. He crashed his snowmobile. Then Lucas came," Jason gushed, barely able to catch his breath. "Lucas said the Spirit Wolf is real."

"Jason, you've just had a bad dream," his father insisted. "I'll get you a glass of water, then try to get back to sleep."

Jason began to cry. "Mom, I heard the Spirit Wolf. I know I did."

He reached into his pajama pocket. "Where is my dream catcher?"

He began frantically searching around the bed.

"I hung it on the wall," his mother replied, "just over your head."

She took it down, slid it into his pocket, gave him a drink of water, and then tucked him back under the covers.

"I think you've had enough dreams for one night."

"He's really had a bad night," Abbie said as she crawled back into bed.

Todd kissed her on the cheek. "I can't imagine what's crashing around inside that little head after all the nonsense he's heard."

"Todd?" Abbie asked.

"Yes."

"That man, Lucas, he couldn't have sneaked in here, could he?"

"Abbie, what in the world are you talking about?"

"The floor is all wet next to his bed, and out in the hall, too."

"Don't be ridiculous. It's probably an ice jam on the roof," Todd mumbled, already half asleep. "This place isn't well insulated. Snow's probably melting around the chimney, backing up under the shingles. Go back to sleep.

Chapter Nine

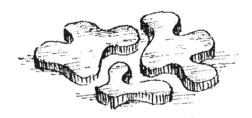

Jason could hear his father's electric coffee grinder whining away in the kitchen. He knew it was Christmas morning and time to get up. He'd been awake for a while, just lying there, trying to make sense of what had happened—or hadn't happened—last night.

I know I was dreaming about the Spirit Wolf, the chase, and the snowmobile crash, Jason thought. *But Lucas was here. I know he is real. He said the Spirit Wolf would help me. I know he did.*

He stepped tentatively onto the cold floor and found the doorway, this time without stumbling into the dresser.

"Jason's up," his mother announced cheerfully. "Merry Christmas."

"Merry Christmas," he replied sleepily. "What time is it anyway?"

"It's almost eight," his father replied.

"The floor's all wet in my room and out in the hall," Jason said.

"Just a roof leak," his father replied. "How are you feeling?"

"I'm okay, I guess," Jason answered. "I've got a little headache, that's all."

"You gave us a bit of a scare last night," his father said.

"I wasn't dreaming, Dad."

"Jason, your mother thought coming here for Christmas would be good for all of us, but I'm afraid we didn't know what we'd be getting into."

"What your father is trying to say," his mother began, "is that the mountains, the lodge, even this little cabin—well, it's just an incredibly beautiful place."

"But these people," his father interrupted, "they're filling your head with a bunch of horse—"

"Please, Todd," his mother pleaded.

"- - dung."

He got up and poked at the fire.

"Please don't think there's some miracle cure for your blindness, that some angel is going to drop out of the sky and give you your sight back," his father continued. "You know, I know, your mother knows what the doctors told us. Some healing may occur, someday. But until that happens, we have to play with the hand we've been dealt. Please try to understand that."

"The Spirit Wolf is real. I heard it," Jason insisted. "Lucas told me the Spirit Wolf would share its magic with me."

"Oh, Jason," his mother cried. "You had a bad dream, that's all. There was no one in your room last night."

She looked away into the fire. She really wasn't sure of anything anymore.

This man, Lucas, couldn't have possibly been in Jason's room, could he?

She was beginning to feel like they'd stepped into a Stephen King novel. Jason seemed almost possessed by this Spirit Wolf, or whatever it was. She thought about leaving for home, right after they opened their gifts. But that might agitate Jason even more, she decided.

"Kate Boone said they open Christmas gifts at nine," she said, trying to break the glum mood. "We'd better get a move on."

The storm had passed. The new snow glittered in the bright morning sun. Jason walked with his mother. Todd followed, his arms wrapped around two plastic shopping bags stuffed with Christmas presents.

Cr-r-ruck. Cr-r-ruck.

"It's the raven again," Jason shouted.

"Probably wishing you a Merry Christmas," his father offered halfheartedly.

The raven called once more, than flew off across the lake.

Jason stopped suddenly, yanking at his mother's elbow.

"What is it, Jason, that wolf again?" she asked.

"No, something's coming. A plane or something."

Now Abbie and Todd heard it—a dull thumping sound.

As they looked up, an olive green helicopter thundered over them, just above the treetops.

"Wow!" Jason shouted. "What was that?"

"That's the helicopter from Fort Drum," his father replied. "Must be looking for Delmonte."

"He went into a river when his snowmobile crashed," Jason said. "They should look there."

"How do you know that?" his father asked.

"It was in my dream."

By the time they reached the lodge, the helicopter had landed on the lake next to the dock. Its blades were still turning. Several men with snowmobiles were standing nearby. Noah Boone was on the front porch.

"What's happening?" Todd asked.

"They found Big Tony a few minutes ago. He's had a rough night: some frost bite, that sort of thing. Tina and Joey are going to accompany him to the hospital in Watertown."

"Where'd they find him?" Todd asked.

"Up on the Cedar River."

Todd and Abbie looked wide-eyed at Jason, then at each other.

"I told you guys," Jason boasted.

"No idea how he ended up there," Noah continued. "He's sopping wet. Why he didn't freeze to death beats me. Sergeant Mead, the flight medic, said he'd call us with an update later today."

Noah headed for the lodge door. "Big Tony must have a guardian angel out there somewhere."

Jody Boone greeted them in the lobby. "Merry Christmas everyone."

She was dressed in a scarlet red sweater, evergreen corduroy pants, and a red and white stocking cap. She bent down and kissed Jason on the cheek. "And a very Merry Christmas to you, Jason."

They walked into the living room. Jody pointed out a small buffet table with juice, coffee, and fresh-baked muffins. Tib Noonan and his wife, Liz Blackstone, and three other women were talking near the Christmas tree. Todd recognized several other faces from the dining room last night. Charlie Two Shirts was tending the fire.

"I'll put our gifts under the tree," Todd said.

Abbie filled two coffee mugs and poured Jason some orange juice. Four men in snowmobile suits trudged through the door and headed for the coffee pot.

"Who are the snowmobilers?" Jason asked.

Abbie couldn't hide her surprise. "How do you know they're snowmobilers?" she asked.

"They always smell oily," Jason replied.

Abbie took a closer look. They were rough-looking men, she thought. The skin on their faces was leather-like, their eyes glazed and pink-veined, as if they'd been on a three-day binge. Perhaps they had. They peeled off the tops of their insulated suits and sat down in the far corner of the room.

"Take a look at what just walked in," she whispered to Todd.

He turned just as one of the men pulled a small flask from his hip pocket. The man spiked his coffee with whatever was in the flask, then passed it to his companions.

"Why didn't I think of that?" Todd whispered back.

Abbie elbowed him in the ribs.

Noah Boone entered the room. "Welcome and a very Merry Christmas. We're so happy to have you with us to celebrate Christmas with our family. As most of you know, Tony Delmonte was rescued just about an hour ago."

A cheer went up around the room.

"We're thankful Big Tony is alive. We'll know more later today."

There was a boisterous round of applause for Bushy. Dressed as Santa, he sunk into a red, high-backed chair by the Christmas tree.

"And now, if my helper will hand me the first gift, we can get started," he chuckled.

Jody reached into a pile of brightly-wrapped boxes. "The first gift is for...Jason!"

There was a loud cheer.

Jason couldn't imagine what it would be like to open Christmas gifts he couldn't see. But tearing away at the foil wrapping, he decided it was still fun. He reached into a shoe-size box. There was something smooth and round, a headset, and some plastic wrapped packages.

"A new Walkman!" he shouted, "and five CD's."

"It's a collection called **Nature's Voices**," his mother added. "It even has whale calls."

Jody continued distributing gifts from family to family. Tib Noonan practiced casting with his new fly rod as soon as it was unwrapped. A blonde-haired woman Abbie hadn't seen before said she'd always wanted a pink flamingo for her front yard. Abbie hoped she was joking.

She and Todd exchanged gifts next: three new Hummel dolls for her, a Tom Clancey book collection for him. Jason opened two more gifts: a hooded winter jacket and two wool sweaters.

As the gift exchange continued, Todd glanced over his shoulder. The four men were passing the flask again. This time they skipped the coffee.

Jody looked around the Christmas tree. "That's about it, folks. How about a nice hand for Santa?"

Everyone cheered. The room began to clear.

"It's just ten-thirty," she added. "Christmas dinner will be served at noon."

"Wait a minute," Bushy said, nosing around the back of the tree. "Looks like we missed one."

He picked up an odd looking, purse-sized string bag. It was made of wool cloth, as if it had been cut from an old coat. The top was stitched with leather bootlaces. There was no ribbon or bow, but there was a hand-written card. Bushy looked at it for a moment, then smiled.

"It's for Jason!"

Todd and Abbie exchanged quizzical looks.

Jason untied the laces and dug into the bag. Even the men sharing the flask stepped forward for a better look.

"What is it?" his mother asked.

"I don't know," Jason replied. "It's filled with little pieces of something."

He took out one, then another. None were shaped the same.

"It feels like...a puzzle," he stammered.

"Let me see that," his father snarled as he took a handful of brightly colored chip-like pieces from the bag. "It's a damn jigsaw puzzle."

"A puzzle?" Abbie gasped.

"What a dreadful gift," Liz Blackstone sighed.

"Who'd give a puzzle to a blind kid?" one of the men in the back shouted.

Jason knew immediately. His heart was broken.

Lucas lied to me, he thought.

He grabbed a handful of the puzzle pieces and rolled them in his hands. There was no magic, no energy, no Spirit Wolf. It had all been a lie. He began to cry.

Charlie Two Shirts started it all with his bag of bones, or whatever it was. Why did he, everyone, play such a trick on me?

"I wonder if that dreadful man who was here last night had anything to do with this," the blonde-haired woman said.

Jason remained silent. He'd never felt so alone.

"Hey, wait a minute," the man with the flask shouted. He was a jowly, pudding-faced man with an immense, pock-scarred nose. "When we rode in this morning, we saw some shaggy—looking guy on snowshoes. Looked like he was heading for Loon Island."

"Who's that?" Abbie whispered to Jody.

"They call him Frog," she replied. "He's a fixture at the Parker House bar."

Frog stepped forward. "If that guy is jerking the kid around, Moose will get it out of him, right, Moose?" Frog said, slapping a hulking, stoop-shouldered man on the back.

The man smiled. His teeth were rotted and tobacco- stained.

Noah raised his hands. "Now hold on, boys. Let's not overreact. We really don't know what this is all about."

Frog began zipping up his snowmobile suit. The others followed.

"We're going to ride out to the island," Frog said. "Have a look; that's all."

The room began to clear. Jason sat in his chair. There were puzzle pieces in his lap and scattered on the floor.

"Let's get our things," his father said. "We're heading for home."

"No, I don't want to go home yet," Jason replied.

"What?" his father asked. "You've been humiliated by this creep. We all have. Come on, Abbie."

The longer Jason sat, the more convinced he became that Charlie Two Shirts wouldn't hurt him. But he couldn't understand the puzzle. Why would Lucas give it to him?

"You've had quite a morning, partner." It was Bushy.

"Do you know where Charlie is?" Jason asked.

"I think he headed back to his place," Bushy began. "I've got to run out to the chapel for a few chores. Want to ride along?"

His father was about to object when Abbie took him aside. "I don't know what's going on, but I can't believe these people could be so cruel. Let him go, Todd, please."

"Go ahead, Jason," his father replied. "We'll be packed when you get back. We'll leave right after dinner."

Bushy put the puzzle pieces back in the wool bag. He and Jason headed out the back door.

Todd gathered up their gifts. He met Abbie at the top of the lodge steps.

"I wish we'd never come here," he said. "That puzzle was such a slap in the face."

Abbie looked out over the lake. "I think it's connected to all this, somehow."

"Connected to what?" Todd asked.

"Well, for starters, Jason's convinced he heard that wolf not once, but three times. You know he hears things we never do."

"Come on, Abbie."

146

"Think about it, Todd," she continued. "Bushy Barnes, Charlie Two Shirts, Father Mulcahy, and this man, Lucas, just walking out of a storm, and all of them saying pretty much the same thing about God and nature. Maybe there is something out there. We just can't feel it."

"Oh, Jesus, Abbie!" Todd snapped. "Let's get back to the cabin. It must be five o'clock somewhere. I could use a drink."

They started down the steps.

"You really can't explain the water on the floor last night," she said, "can you? I checked. The ceiling's not leaking."

Todd stopped. He looked out across the lake momentarily. "No, I can't explain it."

They walked the rest of the way in silence.

Bushy spotted the snowshoes. They were sitting by the chapel door. He shut off the snowmobile and grabbed his toolbox. He and Jason walked inside.

"It's Lucas!" Jason shouted. The smell of pine needles was everywhere.

Lucas was sitting by the fireplace. He nodded at Bushy and smiled.

"I knew it was you!" Jason cried. "There are men hunting for you."

"They've gone to Loon Island," Lucas replied.

Jason was surprised. "How did you know that?"

Lucas smiled at Bushy. "I know these things."

Jason waved the wool bag at Lucas' voice. "You gave me this, didn't you? The bag—it's the same as your coat, and it smells the same, too, like pine needles."

"Yes, Jason, I gave you the puzzle," Lucas began. "But don't be angry. Come sit with me next to the fire."

Bushy picked up his toolbox. "I've got some chores out back. I'll leave you fellas alone."

Jason felt Lucas' hand on his shoulder. "Sit here in this chair. Pour the puzzle pieces out on the table in front of you."

"Why should I?" Jason asked. "I can't put the puzzle together. I can't see the pieces. You know that. Why did you give it to me, anyway?"

He began to cry.

"Together we will look beyond what you cannot see," Lucas whispered.

From his voice, Jason guessed that Lucas was standing directly in back of him. He felt Lucas' hands over his own.

"What are you doing?" Jason asked.

He could feel the heat from Lucas' hands pouring up his arms. He felt light-headed.

"Reach out, Jason. Let the energy pour from you to the puzzle."

Jason spread the puzzle out in front of him. His fingers danced from one tiny piece to the next. He felt hopelessly lost. He thought about what Bill told him: *Always listen to your heart.* He tried one piece, then another, then a third, but they wouldn't fit together.

"I can't do this!" he cried out.

Maybe my parents are right. There is no magic power.

Lucas squeezed his hands harder.

I feel things other people can't, Jason told himself, *so why can't I feel where the pieces go?*

He tried two more pieces. They snapped together!

"Good! Good!" Lucas cried. "Try some more."

His fingers moved faster. He was gasping for air. There was a bright flash. It was blue and lasted just an instant.

Did I really see that, or was it like the shooting star?

He quickly snapped three more pieces together. His head was pounding.

What's happening to me, he wondered.

"What are you feeling, Jason?" Lucas asked.

"I feel like I'm on fire. What are you doing to me, Lucas?"

"Oh, it's not me, Jason. The spirit that connects you to the great mystery, to all of life, is pouring through you."

For an instant, he thought he saw the puzzle pieces spread before him. He wondered if it was a dream, like the Spirit Wolf, on the lake.

But the Spirit Wolf is real, isn't it? Didn't Father Mulchay say so?

He snapped four more pieces together! Something was happening. He was shaking. Sweat streamed from his forehead and ran down his face. His eyes burned like fiery coals.

Turtle, Porcupine, Owl and Eagle, all their wisdom, came pouring back. There was a force—energy more powerful than he had ever known—and it was surging through him. His hands moved faster. Nine more pieces fell into place.

Something was taking form in front of him. He blinked. It was still there. No, it was gone. A soft, blue mist began to wash over his eyes. There were flashes of brilliant colors: daffodil yellows, ruby reds, and emerald greens. His hands dashed about the table as one piece after another locked together.

He blinked and rubbed his eyes.

"Am I dreaming, Lucas?" he shouted. "Is this real?"

"Do you believe in the magic of life?" Lucas asked.

"Yes!" Jason screamed.

"Then you are not dreaming," Lucas whispered. "Finish the puzzle."

Lucas released his grip. But Jason's hands continued to fly from one piece of the puzzle to the next. He was on his own. The mist was melting away. The colors that danced across his eyes came slowly into focus. He rubbed his eyes again. The puzzle was complete. He stared at the gleaming yellow eyes that glared back at him from the puzzle. It was a white wolf.

"I can see it, Lucas!" Jason shouted. "It's the Spirit Wolf!"

He spun around, seeing the chapel for the first time. It was smaller than he'd imagined. Then he saw the Spirit Wolf in the stained-glass window. Its haunting eyes flashed in the late morning sun. He looked frantically around the little sanctuary.

"Lucas!" he shouted. "Lucas!"

But the man called Lucas had vanished.

"What the devil is going on?" Bushy yelled as he rushed through the side door.

Bushy did look like Santa Claus, Jason thought. He ran down the aisle toward him.

"Bushy, I can see you. I can see everything!"

Bushy dropped his toolbox and lifted Jason up in his arms. "Well, I'll be."

"Lucas helped me. It's the puzzle!"

Jason took Bushy's arm and pulled him to the table. "Look, it's the same as the window. It's the Spirit Wolf."

Bushy sat down, pulled a red checkered handkerchief from his overalls, and wiped the sweat running down his forehead.

"Looks like you could use a little wipe, too."

He took a dry corner and wiped the tears from Jason's eyes. "Well now, there must be something to that legend after all," he said with a wink.

Jason was laughing and crying at the same time.

"Where did Lucas go, Bushy? Did he leave?"

They opened the front door. The snowshoes were gone.

151

"I never...saw him," Jason said. "He was real, wasn't he, Bushy?"

"He shared his magic with you, Jason, because you believed he was real. That's all that matters," Bushy replied. "It's coming up on noon. We'd better get you back to your parents. They're in for, well, quite a surprise!"

The snowmobile ride back to the lodge took Jason through a world he was seeing for the first time. The trees were taller, the snow whiter, and the mountains bigger than he'd imagined. He hadn't seen the sky since his accident. It was robin-egg blue with giant fleece-domed clouds. His eyes began to tear as Bushy picked up speed. But he couldn't close them. He couldn't even blink.

"There's the lodge, just up ahead!" Bushy shouted.

It was much bigger than Jason had pictured it. He watched as puffs of white chimney smoke curled up into the cold sky.

"Look at all the deer!" Jason yelled.

Bushy eased off the gas and pulled up to the front door of the lodge.

"I saw your mom and dad walking in as we crossed the bridge," Bushy said. "Why don't you run in there and give them their Christmas present."

Jason jumped off the snowmobile and raced up the steps into the lodge. He saw his parents standing at the far end of the lobby. They were talking to a tall man with gray hair. Jason wondered if that was Mr. Boone.

"Mom! Dad!" he cried as he ran toward them across the lobby.

"Slow down, Jason!" his father shouted. "You'll get hurt."

The commotion woke Rusty, the Boone's aging golden retriever. He ambled from the living room into the middle of the lobby to see what all the excitement was about. Jason jumped to his right, deftly sidestepping the dog, never breaking stride.

"Did you see that!" his mother screamed. "He saw the dog!"

"How...how could he?" his father stammered.

"I can see, Mom! I can see you too, Dad!"

Jason reached his mother's arms as she broke into tears.

"I don't believe it," his father cried. "What happened? How did you...," his voice trailed off as he searched for words he couldn't find.

"It was Lucas...the puzzle...the Spirit Wolf!" Jason gasped. He tried to tell his parents what happened, but the words just kept coming too fast.

The news spread quickly through the lodge. In the living room, where guests were gathered before dinner, Jason was the center of attention. Todd refused to believe his son's miraculous healing was the result of some mystical, magical intervention. He spotted Tib Noonan and went looking for another answer.

"Dr. Noonan, you've heard my son's explanation. What do you make of it?"

Tib Noonan was a wispy, gray-haired man. His half-sized reading glasses were fashionably perched on the tip of his long, pink nose. He took a puff from his pipe. Smoking was not permitted in the lodge, but Dr. Tibb Noonan of Manhattan appeared to have a dispensation from Noah Boone's ironclad rules.

"The body can cure itself of many illnesses," he began. "I understand the lad's condition was cortical blindness. It can reverse itself over time, if the nerve endings heal. My guess is that's precisely what has happened. It occurring all at once on Christmas Day, well, that's just an ironic coincidence."

"Then you don't believe in miracles," Abbie said. "Is that it, Dr. Noonan?"

Jason was standing nearby. "You don't believe in the Spirit Wolf?"

"Well, there is an alternative school of thought."

He took another puff from his pipe. He was clearly amused as he watched the smoke curl up toward the ceiling. He loved an audience. And he loved breaking Noah Boone's rules.

"There is a fringe out there, a few doctors, who believe the human spirit and the human body are intimately connected. They believe the mind can correct mistakes or injuries to the body."

He examined his pipe and took another long draw. "Of course, every once in a while, someone is miraculously cured of some terminal condition. No one can explain it."

Noah Boone had been listening. He rubbed his chin. "Well, some things, at least for now, are best left unexplained. Magic does happen, you know."

The front door swung open. It was Frog, closely followed by Moose and the two other men. Their snowmobile suits were caked with ice.

"Well, did you find that weirdo?" the blonde woman asked.

Jason smiled quietly to himself.

"We rode out to Loon Island, where he was supposed to be camping," Frog replied.

Someone handed him a Labatt's. He quickly drained half the bottle. Liz Blackstone winced when he finished with a tumultuous belch.

"There was no camp, not a sign of any camp. All we found were coyote tracks. Biggest I ever seen. Now Fritz here, he's from Canada," Frog continued, pointing to one of his companions. "Fritz says they was wolf tracks."

A cadaverous, bean pole of a man with hollowed eyes and crinkled nose punched Frog on the arm. "I knows a wolf track when I sees one," he said confidently.

"Sure, Fritz, sure," Frog continued. "We followed the tracks out across the lake, but they just disappeared, like the damn thing, whatever it was, just jumped up in the air and never came down."

He polished off his beer. Moose immediately handed him another.

Kate Boone hung up the office phone and walked briskly into the living room.

"That was the helicopter medic," she began. "He said Big Tony's going to be okay. I guess he was hallucinating all the way to Watertown. He claimed he was chasing a white wolf when he hit the Cedar River Trail barrier, ended up in the river, and was lucky to get out. About midnight he thought he was a goner. He was getting numb and real sleepy. He said he made himself a promise that if he ever got out alive, he was never coming back to the Adirondacks again. Just then, some shabby- looking guy on snowshoes comes out of nowhere, gets a fire going for him, and tells him someone will be by for him in the morning. Then the guy just...disappeared."

"Lucas?" everyone in the room seemed to whisper at the same time.

"Maybe this puts an end to the Osprey Project," Jody ventured.

"Let's hope so," Noah replied. "Maybe the Seven Peaks Wilderness has a chance after all."

Jody rang the silver bell that hung just outside the dining room. "Come and get it, everyone!" she called out.

The living room began to clear.

"Can I catch up with you guys in the dining room?" Jason asked his parents. "I'd like to look around for just a minute or two."

"Sure," his father replied. "Look around all you like."

Jason walked out onto the porch. He covered his eyes momentarily in the blinding sunlight. He didn't need his jacket. The wind was still and the sun warm. He stuck out his tongue and sipped from the melting icicles that hung from the porch roof like giant stalactites at the mouth of an icy cave. The mountains were brushed in a plum-gray wash. There were occasional splashes of sage green where hardwoods gave way to needled spruce and white pine. He took a deep breath and stared off across the lake.

"The mountains have opened your eyes."

Jason recognized the voice immediately. He turned and saw Charlie Two Shirts for the first time. He was much taller than he'd guessed, and his skin was lighter. Jason ran to Charlie's side and buried his head in his smoky wool shirt.

"Do you remember what Father Mulcahy asked you last night?" Charlie asked.

"About…angels?"

"That's right."

Jason looked for the first time into Charlie's coal black eyes.

"Was Lucas an angel?"

Charlie swept his arms out toward the lake. "Angels are all around us, Jason. They take many forms. Their medicine is strong. You know that now."

"Was Lucas the Spirit Wolf?"

"The Spirit Wolf lives in the hearts of everyone who believes there is a force greater than our own. It is a force so strong that it flows from these mountains and surrounds us with its magic."

Jason gave Charlie a long hug and headed back inside. He was about to close the door when he heard it. The wolf's call began with a single note. It rose sharply, then rolled across the lake. It was a wild, distant cry that echoed off the distant mountains.

Jason ran back onto the porch and looked out over the lake. He was sure he saw it, a ghostlike silhouette, its legs barely moving, floating like fog over the snow. And then it was gone.